Praise for *Arborescence*:

'You will not be able to stop thinking about this extraordinary book. A thrilling page-turner for our times, one that chills and provokes' Sophie Ward, author of *Love and Other Thought Experiments*

'A great and beautiful book that is profound and profoundly moving. Airy, light, witty, with the frankness of a Sally Rooney novel and the delicate strangeness of Olga Tokarczuk. I couldn't have been more entranced' Jennifer Croft, author of *Homesick*

'As absurd as it is utterly convincing, this is a book about holding onto love in a world of seismically shifting reality. In other words, a book about us, a book about now. It's brilliant' Shaun Tan, author of *Tales of Light and Dark*

'Original, mind-bending and uplifting. I loved this beautiful, feral book so much, I wanted to walk into its pages and never look back' Inga Simpson, author of *The Thinning*

'A strange and compelling exploration of our current moment. *Arborescence* is part Sally Rooney, part Stephen King. It reads like a thriller but has the tenderness and insight of poetry' Ben Rawlence, author of *The Treeline*

'A balm and an urgent whisper of hope. This is a book to help us believe that all is not lost. Extraordinary' Kate Mildenhall, author of *The Hummingbird Effect*

'Thrilling, thought-provoking, and incredibly tender ... I devoured it whole' Chioma Okereke, author of *Water Baby*

'Intelligent and thoughtful ... a dystopian world that feels simultaneously too close to home and impossibly science fiction, yet leaves you with an almost utopian feeling of solace and optimism. A philosophical book about the very nature of being human and the future of our species, but also a personal story of love, loss, and redemption' Lisa Ridzén, author of *When the Cranes Fly South*

'Inventive ... a generous act of writing ... If you're looking for something that's clever, that won't bum you out, that's beautifully written, then this might be the one for you' ABC Radio National

'*Arborescence* is speculative fiction at its best: an end-of-world story that offers green leaves of hope' *ArtsHub*

'Prepare yourself for a weird one ... Rhett Davis is a skilled and playful writer with an eye for the absurd and the profound ... an unforgettable tale' *Qantas Magazine*

'Davis' signature narrative playfulness and dryly humorous dialogue is always on hand to help sweep us further into the story ... *Arborescence* is a reminder of the special way fictional worlds can allow readers to retreat from, and find the fortitude to return to, their own world' *The Age*

'Intriguing, utterly original ... leaves a lasting impression and rings with unsettling questions' Readings, Book of the Month

'With Davis' sharp eye and irreverent humour, the genre-blurring story branches into the tangled roots of suburban life and the natural world' *Sydney Morning Herald*

'I did not know how much I needed a novel like *Arborescence*. On one level, it's a beguiling story about humans who metamorphose to save the warming planet. On another level, it's a *cri de coeur*, written with tenderness for all who wonder how this ends. A tremendously moving affirmation of what's worth saving – love, family, clean air, and silence. I wept through the last fifty pages' Amity Gaige, author of *Heartwood*

'A dazzling blend of cosmic eco-horror and arthouse sci-fi, *Arborescence* is one of the most profound and beautiful books you'll ever read. A devastating and unforgettable elegy for the planet' Chris Flynn, author of *Orpheus Nine*

ARBORESCENCE

RHETT DAVIS

FLEET

FLEET

First published in Australia and New Zealand by Hachette Australia in 2025
First published in Great Britain in 2026 by Fleet

1 3 5 7 9 10 8 6 4 2

Copyright © Rhett Davis 2025

The moral right of the author has been asserted.

*All characters and events in this publication, other than those
clearly in the public domain, are fictitious and any resemblance
to real persons, living or dead, is purely coincidental.*

All rights reserved.
No part of this publication may be reproduced, stored in a
retrieval system, or transmitted, in any form, or by any means, without
the prior permission in writing of the publisher, nor be otherwise circulated
in any form of binding or cover other than that in which it is published
and without a similar condition including this condition being
imposed on the subsequent purchaser.

A CIP catalogue record for this book
is available from the British Library.

Hardback ISBN 978-0-349-72530-7
Trade paperback ISBN 978-0-349-72531-4

Author photograph courtesy of Julian Dolman
Typeset in 11/17 pt Adobe Caslon Pro by Bookhouse, Sydney
Printed and bound in Great Britain by Clays Ltd, Elcograf S.p.A.

Papers used by Fleet are from well-managed forests
and other responsible sources.

Fleet
An imprint of
Little, Brown Book Group
Carmelite House
50 Victoria Embankment
London EC4Y 0DZ

The authorised representative
in the EEA is
Hachette Ireland
8 Castlecourt Centre
Dublin 15, D15 XTP3, Ireland
(email: info@hbgi.ie)

An Hachette UK Company
www.hachette.co.uk

www.littlebrown.co.uk

FOR BEN, BROOKE, AND TARA

To hell with machinery.

Kurt Vonnegut, *Conversations with Kurt Vonnegut*

It's been days and she hasn't moved. She just stands in the backyard. She says she doesn't need anything, that she's drawing water from the air and the ground and her energy from the sun. Last night it rained and I begged her to come inside. She shook her head slowly, as if doing so caused her pain. I took out an umbrella and held it over her, but she growled so deeply and inhumanly that I dropped it and fled inside.

In the morning, Travis comes around and I make coffee. We sit down next to her, hoping the aroma will tempt her.

It doesn't.

'She's given up,' Travis says.

'That's not what this is,' I say.

1

Caelyn takes a deep breath and sneezes. 'The pollen count is up,' she says, as she tries to salvage her desiccated monstera by drowning it. 'Like, way, way up.'

I'm watching a video my brother, Travis, has sent me. It's of some people standing in a field somewhere, facing the sun. There's no punchline. No-one falls down. They just stand there. The video goes for three hours. I don't know why he sends me these things.

'Fuck,' Caelyn says, as water pours out of the base of the pot and onto the floor. She doesn't move.

I grab some towels and mop up.

She sighs and rubs her eyes. 'Hey,' she says, 'are my eyes red?'

'I'm going to need more towels,' I say.

'Bren, how red are they?'

I look up. Beyond her bloodshot blue eyes and sniffling nose, I can see – in the shafts of sunlight that stream into our third-floor apartment – particles swirling, wisping, arms reaching, grasping, circling her head.

—

At the pub, Travis asks if we watched the video of the tree cult.

We're in the beer garden, sunglasses on, chattering, calling, texting. The sun has emerged after months of searching for a way through thick winter cloud. It's a fierce light and it bites the skin.

I shake my head and say, 'Mum asked me about Miles again.'

Travis says, 'It's been years.'

'We weren't even friends anymore.'

'I reckon she liked him more than you. Always gave him bigger serves of ice cream.'

'Bigger than yours, too.'

He shakes his head. 'Nah, she always gave me heaps of ice cream.'

Caelyn says, 'What's this tree cult video?'

Mel rolls her eyes and says, 'It's just performance art. It happens all the time where I'm from – people coming from the city and doing this sort of wacky shit. Until the farmers get sick of it and chase them off. I'm getting a round.' She points at each of us. I decline. My glass is half full and I can hear but can't see bees, both of which suggest I should take it slowly. Mel says that I'm nursing it, and I say that nursing is a noble profession. She waves me away and goes up to the bar.

Travis says, 'There's like thirty people standing around near some forest out west. Standing there like they think they're trees. It's weird. Doesn't look like art to me.'

Mel comes back, somehow holding four pints, and puts a fresh one in front of me. I point to the one I'm holding and ask if anyone can hear bees.

—

'I've never finished anything I've set out to do,' Caelyn murmurs, contemplating the unfinished projects, ideas, sketches on her desk.

'That's not true,' I say, but I don't have much to back it up, so I pretend I'm bothered by an article about the fall of capitalism. As it turns out, capitalism refuses to die. They come up with all sorts of other names for it, try to claim it's something else now, something worse.

'It doesn't matter what it's called,' she says, momentarily distracted from her crisis. 'We'll still eat the earth until there's nothing left. I wish aliens would invade.'

—

I click on the next work package in the Queue. *Describe this product*, the Queue demands. I open the attached image to see a device made of plastic, or perhaps resin. There might be a flower in it. Visible screws either hold it together or are there for aesthetic reasons. I think there's a clasp.

'What is this for?' I say – to no-one, because Caelyn's at interviews again and Henry, the kitten we rescued from the back of a supermarket, is in one of his haughtier moods.

I don't know much about the company I work for. I joined three years ago, six months after graduating. They don't have a physical address, and I've never met anyone in person. I'm a Queue Liaison. I log in to the Queue every weekday. It grows and grows, a little like a tree, and my job is to lop off as many branches as I can. It's hard to see a trend, to understand what it's all for. The mission statement of the company reads like every mission statement ever created. We *further progress*, and *forward innovate for maximum creative enterprise*, among other things. Sometimes I'll be writing copy for products, other times generating code for an interface, interpreting an algorithm, creating a funny image for social media or a self-published cookbook, or editing a plan to remove inappropriate references because the conversation has changed. I rarely know the context. Who is this for, what is it for? But I trim the Queue, I get paid on time, and every few weeks my manager sends me messages like, *With this kind of velocity you'll be doing my job in no time.*

Whatever it is we're doing, there's little humanity in it.

—

Caelyn says she's accepted a job in a garden centre.

I say, 'I didn't know you'd applied.'

She says she loves plants.

'I know you *like* plants,' I reply. 'I just wouldn't say you *love* them.' I add, 'That reminds me: we need more towels.'

'I love plants,' she repeats, gently touching the leaves of our dying indoor palm tree. 'Anyway,' she says, 'this is just temporary. Until I work out what I want to do.' She's had sixteen jobs in our four years together.

I say, 'Everything's temporary.'

She glares at me and says with a hint of malice, 'Yes, it is.'

—

I dream of the Queue, but instead of a tree it resembles vines emerging from the earth, wrapping themselves around me, squeezing my throat. I wake up coughing and wrestling with Caelyn's mass of red hair, which is covering my face. She hands me her asthma inhaler and mumbles, 'It's the pollen.'

—

'The day we met,' Caelyn says, as we browse the homewares department, 'you were holding a sunflower. You took it to all your classes.'

'It was Mother's Day,' I say.

'But I don't understand why you didn't just get the sunflower afterward?'

'It got your attention.'

She shakes her head. 'That wasn't what got my attention.' She picks up a small figurine of a family of penguins. 'This'll do, don't you think?'

'You know your sister better than me,' I say. 'Wait, what got your attention?'

She frowns. 'You know Morgan almost as well as I do these days. Anyway, it's too hard to buy presents for people with lots of money because they can buy themselves electric cars or whatever, so she's getting penguins.' She buys the penguins and a card with a joke about a uterus I don't really understand.

As we're leaving the store she says, 'You didn't have facial hair.'

'That was it?'

'I dunno. You were tall and you had nice arms.'

'I do have good arms,' I say, admiring them. 'People have often said that.'

'Yeah, I probably wasn't paying that much attention,' she admits.

—

The Queue presents me with a list of current work packages, their category, priority and what is being requested. Every day there's more, and there are thousands of work packages open at any one time.

The next one I'm assigned has an image attached. It's a photograph of a concert ticket in Bruges. The request is to reproduce the image of the ticket as accurately as possible using whatever means I like. I consider this for a moment before taking a screenshot of the ticket and re-attaching the file to the work package. The Queue responds: *Work package accepted. Efficiently executed!*

Caelyn messages me from the garden centre. *According to my new colleague Nancy, plants need sunlight. Did you know this?*

—

After the movie about people with laser eyes saving the world, Travis says, 'What would you sacrifice to save the world?'

Asha says, 'Ooh, I would . . . um. Oh. Um. Ice cream.'

'No fucking way,' Travis says.

Caelyn says, 'I'll only save the world if it means saving the penguins.'

'I don't think anyone would give up anything,' I say. 'When it comes down to it.'

Caelyn slaps my knee in agreement, and Travis says I'm a downer, which is true, but I say his wine is a depressant, and he says yes, but he still thinks we could save the world, and Asha says no-one can save the world, it's all fucked, and Travis looks at all of us in disgust and says, did that movie not teach you that unless we find something to hope for we'll lose everything? It's a self-fulfilling prophecy. Like, without hope, we give up. We stop trying to save anything. We have to have hope. It's our only way out of this. And I nod and say yes, but wine is a depressant and we don't have laser eyes, so.

—

Dad calls and says Mum has started forgetting where her keys are, and I say, 'Dad, I think you're the one who's been doing that,' and he says, 'Right, right. Pain in the arse. Can never remember where I put them. How about the Raiders last night, hey?'

—

When she's sick of screens and the outside world, Caelyn sketches the plants in our apartment. She fills notebooks with leaves, petals, stamens, stigmas and anthers.

—

Mum calls and says they spent thirty minutes that morning searching for the car keys. 'Turns out they were still in his pocket from last night,' she says. 'I was late for my glass-blowing class again. Do you know if Travis has house insurance, love?'

'We rarely find time to talk about insurance these days,' I say.

'Tch. I was just asking.'

'Ask *him*!'

'He doesn't answer my questions,' she says.

'Well, I guess we'll never know.'

'At least until his house burns down. Then we'll know.' She says it as if she's thinking about lighting the match. I'm pretty sure she doesn't mean it that way, but she did symbolically burn my *Dungeons and Dragons* books when she heard that they were a gateway to hard drugs and serial killing, so you never know.

—

'What if,' Caelyn says, putting a box of macaroni back on the supermarket shelf with the tinned tomatoes, 'there's no humanity left in humanity? What if we've become the robots? With our algorithms and all that?'

I say, 'We were talking about rice.'

She says, 'But robots.' She considers the cannellini beans. 'What if you don't need to have cybernetic implants to be a robot, you just have to live in a computer world, which is kind of what we're doing – you know, like we're being told what to do by algorithms and stuff. Like with your job. You're kind of like a robot within a robot.'

I wait for the conclusion, but there is none.

Eventually I say, 'Yes, but I'm going to go get some rice anyway.'

When we get to the register, I pack the groceries. As I scan the barcodes Caelyn whispers in my ear, 'Robots.'

—

Gardenezia, the garden centre where Caelyn works, is on a highway a few kilometres from the city. I find her at the register, closing up, with leaves in her hair. She says, 'Hullo!' as I approach.

'You have leaves in your hair,' I say.

'Oh,' she says.

'Here,' I say, removing a gumnut and some robinia leaves.

She glances toward the office and says loudly, 'Nancy didn't tell me I had plant matter in my hair.'

Nancy, if she's there, doesn't answer.

Caelyn shuts down the registers. She waves her arm at them like she's modelling a showcase on a game show. She says grandly, 'Robots.'

'Let's just go,' I say.

'Also,' she says, after a few kilometres in the dreadful traffic that marks these garden centre suburbs, 'Nancy is a bit of a cunt.'

—

'I want to go back to university,' Caelyn says. 'I like it there. The weird architecture, the terrible cafes, the young people all full of hope or terror or whatever.'

Morgan stirs her coffee and says, 'What good's another degree? You can't even pay off your arts degree.'

Normally I prefer not to attend these sisterly meet-ups, but I couldn't come up with an excuse.

'I like university,' Caelyn says. 'I'm just saying I like university.'

Morgan gives her the pitying older sister look. 'Oh, sis,' she says, 'you need a purpose. Don't you think she needs a purpose, Bren?'

I excuse myself and investigate the cakes.

—

'Also,' Caelyn says, as we wander home from the cafe along streets lined with lemon-scented gums, 'Morgan is a bit of a cunt.'

—

'Maybe I'll write an article,' Caelyn says.

'What about?' I say.

'I don't know,' she says. 'I don't know.' And her eyes begin to well up and her cheeks begin to burn and she says, 'I don't know, I don't know,' and she crumples onto the couch, causing Henry to dramatically flee the room.

I pick her up and try to hold her but her body is limp and she refuses to hold me back. I let her fall gently back down.

'I would really like to know,' she sobs.

I say, 'I know you would like to know. We'd all like to know. But maybe true knowing isn't something we ever know.'

She looks up at me. Her freckly face is raw and there's snot in her hair. It's disgusting. She wipes her face with her sleeve. 'I know you think you're being funny and unhelpful to try to distract me, but that's actually quite insightful,' she says.

—

'Ray was asking about you,' Mum says, as she pours the gin and tonic. 'They still haven't heard from Miles.'

She hands me the drink and we go out into the backyard. Dad's busy with the secateurs. We sit next to the lemon tree they planted when they moved in thirty years ago. Mum and Dad bought the place before Travis and I were born and have never stopped renovating it. There are always new rooms, new floors, new windows. When we were growing up, we often had to move out of our bedrooms for a few weeks so that Dad could put down flooring or repaint. After we left home they added a storey. The new rooms have very little purpose. They're just up there, above the rest of the house, with an occasional couch or dartboard.

'He's been missing six years, Mum,' I say. 'He's gone.'

She puts her hand on my arm, the way she does when she's trying to get me to respond in a more emotionally appropriate way. I must have a problem responding appropriately because she does this often. 'Miles is their son, Bren. They'll never stop looking. You haven't heard anything?'

I take a sip and recoil at the liberal usage of gin. 'No,' I say. 'We still aren't speaking.'

Mum tuts. 'Neil,' she says, 'don't cut them back too far. You know what happened last time.'

—

The bees seem happy about the high pollen count – when I can see them.

—

'I'm watching that tree cult video again,' Caelyn says. 'The one that Travis sent us the other day.'

As usual, I nod before I know what's happening. Oh yes, we talked about it in the pub. People standing in a field. Boring.

'Travis was right,' she says. 'It doesn't feel like they're performing. They think they're trees.'

Her phone, perched precariously next to the stovetop as she cooks, shows the video about two hours in. The people are still standing there.

'It's strange,' she says. 'Almost serene.'

I say that I think everything is strange, the entire world is one strange thing that shouldn't exist, like what are we even doing here at all, how are trees even a thing, what is movement?

She keeps stirring the pot and watching the video.

'Are you sure you don't need help with that?' I say, and she says, 'Yes, I know, but I'm just talking about this particular strange thing.'

—

The Queue sends me another work package, another product to describe. There is plastic, and some fur, pink and vertical, like the hair on those Norwegian trolls. There might be eyes, but I'm not entirely sure it's a creature. It could be a character from some obscure anime I know nothing about. It could also be a wine stopper. There's really no way of knowing. I write something about the ceaseless march of time and move on to the next job. I've never had any feedback about the quality of my work, just an acknowledgement that it's been completed.

'The world's not looking good,' I say, and Dad says, 'Are you going to finish that?'

—

I walk by a neighbour's place most afternoons. She plays violin – not badly, but not well. Stilted fragments emerge from the house. A first bar, a half-song, a cluster of broken notes. Sudden halts and long pauses. Then she starts again. And again. I see her at the supermarket sometimes. She buys gluten-free pasta and a lot of chocolate. That's really all I know about her. But sometimes when I walk past her place she gets it right, all the way through, and her music fills the street. The nearby buildings, trees and people all lean closer.

—

There's a man who goes to the cafe I usually visit. He's always dressed in a suit. Neko, the cafe owner, calls him AJ, but I don't know if that's his name. He comes in one morning, shirt untucked and looking frazzled, and orders a strong coffee. I hear Neko say, 'You alright, AJ? A little out of sorts, mate?'

AJ doesn't appear to be listening. He looks out the window and says, 'Did you know there's a place not far away where people are trees?'

The espresso machine bursts with steam and Neko laughs. 'What are you talking about, mate?'

AJ continues looking out the window at the morning sun streaming in. 'Wouldn't it be nice just standing there, not moving, feeling the sun on your face and the earth at your feet?' he says.

Neko hands him his coffee and says, 'I put an extra shot in there today. Might help.'

I watch AJ shuffle off dreamily, coffee in hand. I go back to validating code to fix the output of a virtual object whose purpose I don't know.

—

On the train station wall there's an enormous mural of a beautiful woman, weeping. Underneath, the artist has spray-painted in large letters, *THERE IS NO HOPE*. Underneath that, someone else has painted in more frantic, less aesthetically pleasing letters, *You don't know shit, Patrick.*

—

Both Caelyn and Henry kill spiders with glee. If I see one creeping around the house, I quickly grab a sheet of paper and a glass and stealthily move it to the balcony outside, where a more natural death almost certainly awaits it. But for a moment the spider and I are connected in a fight for its life, and I feel the terror of the prey, waiting for the hunter to wake from its slumber on its sunlit couch, knock it to the ground and crush it with a paw.

—

Caelyn brings home another plant. She takes the ones the garden centre is going to throw out. She's only been working there for a few weeks, but we have about fifty now. Their vines and leaves cover our walls, shelves and windows. They're all in various stages of distress. Henry takes one look and runs underneath our bed. He won't emerge for hours, and when he does, it'll be to sniff and swat every leaf that he can see.

Caelyn asks me where she should put the new plant. I say there's probably a spare bit of ceiling somewhere. Unfortunately she nods in agreement. She spends the next hour balanced on a ladder, banging things into the ceiling.

—

'We've done this to ourselves,' Caelyn says, as she pulls into the petrol station. Sometimes she'll go for hours without saying anything and then say something like this, as if I've been following the conversation in her head.

'Are you talking about humanity in general or the fact that we should have filled up earlier?' I say.

'Both,' she says, and gets out of the car.

—

She shares a video of an old cartoon. An army of trees, led by one wearing a military beret, marches toward a city. *THEY ARE COMING*, says the caption at the end.

'Why did you send that?' I call across the apartment.

'I don't know,' she yells back.

I watch it a few times. She walks into the lounge room with Henry in her arms and flops down next to me. The cat wriggles out of her grip and runs away. At the doorway he considers us with contempt before disappearing.

'He does love me,' she says.

'There's no evidence of that,' I say.

'Pfft,' she says.

—

We watch *The Lord of the Rings*, and after it's over, she rewinds to the part when the forest eats the Orcs in Helm's Deep, saying, 'I love this bit.'

—

'Look at this,' Caelyn says, showing me her phone.

'It's the middle of the night,' I say. 'Go to sleep.'

She shoves the phone in my face. 'It's another tree video.'

I squint at the screen. A video plays of people standing still in a field ringed by bushland, eyes closed.

'It's just another bunch of people standing there,' I say.

She says, 'Yes, another group. This looks like it could be near one of the forests outside the city, though. Look, there are mountain ash. Maybe I could write an article about that?'

I sigh and turn over, away from the glare of the phone. 'Sure,' I say, perhaps too hastily. You never know when a mumbled affirmation will change the course of your life.

—

The next morning she says she's going to do it.

'Do what?' I ask.

'The article I was talking about,' she says.

I nod and say, 'Hmm,' and concentrate on stirring my coffee.

'I was talking to you about it last night,' she says. 'The one about the tree cult. That local group. I found some of their family members on social media, and they pretty much posted where they are; it's not far from here. We used to camp nearby when we were kids. I'll need to go visit. Although a bunch of people standing around believing they're trees does feel a little, I don't know, murder-y. Maybe you could come?'

I keep stirring my coffee. I stall for as long as I can. The article, I think. The tree cult, I think. 'Oh,' I say. 'The cult. The article. Um, what about work?'

She grimaces and sucks in a breath through clenched teeth. 'They, ah, fired me.'

I stop stirring and look up at her. 'What? Why?'

She shifts uncomfortably in her chair. 'Well,' she says, 'apparently the plants weren't actually for me to take. They weren't going to throw them out. Even though they were totally going to throw them out. They have some sort of arrangement with the council or something. I just figured they wouldn't mind.'

I glance around the room. Every spare shelf, bookcase, table and wall holds a plant. There's no room to sit on the balcony. There are ferns, ivies, figs, orchids, rubber plants, succulents and other leafy things I don't recognise. Most of them are looking worse than when they arrived.

'You stole them?' I say.

She rolls her eyes and says, 'It didn't feel like stealing.'

'Hmm,' I say.

'Hmm,' she says.

We put our backpacks in the car and drive. It takes a long time to reach the far side of the outer suburbs. When we do, the highway cuts through a wide plain. I curate a playlist that would last for a thousand kilometres, or a round-the-world flight. But I keep adding to it anyway. The day is warm and bright, and Caelyn drives with the window down. I look up from the phone and feel, for a moment, something like possibility.

'What do you think makes a person believe they're a tree?' she says.

'Mental illness,' I say.

She shakes her head. 'I don't think a collective delusion like this would exist without a sociopathic figurehead. I bet there's a wanker with a manifesto.'

The plains are wide and treeless with occasional stone walls dividing paddocks from the highway. 'It's hard to believe we'll ever see trees again, looking around here.'

As if I hadn't spoken, she says, 'Yeah. Or maybe they're tired of being mammals, you know? Like they've been on some forum about society needing to slow down or whatever, and they've taken it to a ridiculous level.'

'It's exhausting having muscles and blood and stuff,' I say. 'Being still and peaceful and not having to twitch, fuck and eat sounds nice.'

She frowns. 'I like fucking and eating,' she says.

We pass a lone tree in a field, an old eucalyptus that has been left to grow, farmed around for years.

'I wonder what it'd be like,' I say. 'Being a tree.'

She looks at the road. The highway ahead snakes up through beckoning hills and green rocky fields. Beyond that, according to the map, is the forest. 'When we get there, you should stand next to them for a bit,' she says. 'See how it feels. See if it takes.'

I ask if she's going to steal plants from the cult.

'Don't be a dick,' she says.

I say I'm not being a dick.

'You're being a dick,' she says, and I say, 'Nah,' even though I probably am.

We move into that sulky phase that sometimes afflicts us these days. It is something more than silence; a weight, a tiredness, a burden, an alone-together.

—

Into the hills. At first, pockets of trees, then we plunge into the forest. The late spring sun flickers between tall white trunks of mountain ash. Its ghostly light falls gently over walls of enormous tree ferns. Despite the warmth of the day, a mist embraces us briefly, releasing us a few seconds later. I lower my window. The air is heavy and smells like the freshest, cleanest dirt and the sharp-clear sting of eucalyptus. Something old there too. Ancient, angry.

I say that I'm sorry, and she says for what, and I say, for being a dick and, look, probably everything up to this point, and she says, just breathe, Bren.

She smiles and lowers all the windows and screams.

—

Following the route she meticulously prepared, we turn at an old dirt track that looks as though it hasn't been used for some time. It's full of ruts and small canyons, and seems more like a riverbed than a road. Caelyn turns on the four-wheel drive. I didn't realise our car had four-wheel drive. She drives expertly, navigating each bump carefully.

'Dad used to drive us for hours on these tracks to get to some clearing by a waterfall, or a big rock overlooking a valley.'

I say, 'Uh-huh,' and bounce with the car.

'You nervous?' she says.

'Not at all,' I say. I consider my body for a moment. I appear to be holding the seat tightly. 'I am fairly certain we're going to end up on the news, either murdered or scammed,' I say. 'I packed a cricket bat.'

She laughs and says, 'Hey, the road ends here. There's an old walking track that'll take us the rest of the way.'

She parks the car then gets out, grabs her pack and makes for a barely noticeable trail through the ferns. There's a gentle wind brushing the dizzyingly high treetops, and from somewhere the rushing of water. There are shadows everywhere.

'I'm not sure I like forests,' I call out as I put my pack on. 'I don't like that part of *The Lord of the Rings* at all. It's really terrifying.'

It would be so easy to become lost here. It's an enormous, hostile labyrinth. There's beauty, sure, but also something darker, a drowsy malevolence.

Caelyn, already well ahead of me, doesn't respond.

She always races ahead when we go for hikes. She doesn't look back. She never looks back. Eventually I'll find her perched on a rock, drinking, snacking, or basking in the sun with her eyes closed. She'll spring to life when she sees me, shoulder her pack again, and set off before I've had time to sit and rest. She says she gets energy in bursts, like a cat, and that I'm more of a lumbering beast, like a cow, or an easily startled jumping creature, like an antelope or a rabbit. Prey, in other words. Sometimes she hides in the bushes, waiting for me to approach. Sometimes she waits for me to pass and attacks from behind. Often, she bites.

—

The sound of water flowing, louder now, but from where? Tree ferns the height of two people tower over the path and form a canopy within the canopy. Branches and roots and moss and leaves and peat (or something like peat). The trail keeps winding through it all, climbing and falling. The forest grows even darker, the scent of decay riper. The sunlight barely reaches the ground.

I can feel centuries of earth, of air, of light. A city, a country, a world.

I jump across a puddle of black water. This forest is drawing me in to confuse me, to confound me. My heart races. The trail descends further, the shadows bearing their own shadows. It's not too late to turn around.

—

As I cross a small creek, sunlight bursts through the canopy. On the other side I stop. The water is tea-stained but clear, and I run my hands through it. It's colder than I'd anticipated. I dry my hands on my jacket and try to warm them up with my breath. I feel the hair rising on the back of my neck. I freeze. I can't hear anything other than the water. All prey needs water. The predator waits patiently as their prey follows its predictable paths. The only question is from where –

Something slams into me, pins me to the ground and bites my neck, hard. She continues growling, thrashing and biting until she's had enough, then she stands and says, 'Took you long enough.'

I sit up. 'The forest is like you,' I say. 'A predator. A very patient one.'

'People are the only real predators left,' she says.

—

'That documentary we watched,' she says, as we approach the crest of a hill. More sunlight is seeping through, and the tree ferns have given way to grasses. 'About the guy who made clockwork toys. What was the point of that? Were they being serious and saying this guy was amazing, or was it demonstrating the futility of human endeavours? Because those toys he made were not good. At all.'

'It could have been a satire.'

She turns around and says, 'Yes! But it could have been completely serious. I couldn't work out what I was supposed to do with it.'

'What are you supposed to do with any piece of art?'

'Understand it?'

'That's not the point of art.'

She's about to continue arguing, but instead stops at the top of the hill and gasps.

'What is it?' I say.

She reaches for my shoulder, but it's not there yet. I hurry forward. Her hand finds my shoulder and squeezes.

I follow her gaze. We've arrived at the edge of the forest. Kilometres of grassy fields stretch into the distance, with rolling hills and the remnants of old tree trunks, likely cut down decades ago. The sunlight is suddenly blinding, the feeling of shadowy dread lifted, only to be replaced by another kind: a dread that is desiccated, formless and shapeless.

'Look,' she whispers, 'over there.'

She points to a hill not far away, where around thirty people stand quietly, arms at their sides, several metres apart from each other. They don't move. It is as silent now as it has been the entire journey. A light breeze brushes the grass that covers the otherwise naked hills, a breeze the forest had sheltered us from.

'Is it a protest?' I whisper.

She looks at me blankly. 'A protest,' she says. 'Here. Where no-one can see it.'

'Group meditation?'

'They're trying to become trees, Bren.'

We stare at the people a little while longer. There's no movement at all, just the wind blowing their hair. They face the same direction, their heads slightly tilted upward, to the sky. I'm not sure how they're able to stay still for so long. I can't hold a yoga pose for more than five seconds.

'Maybe they're dead,' I say, 'and they're being held up by stakes. Like Jesus.'

Caelyn says, 'Well, there's one way of finding out.'

She moves toward them, but I grab her arm.

'Wait,' I say.

She considers this briefly before walking off, ignoring my silent, frantic waving. I give up and follow. My skin crawls as we get closer.

We pause a couple of metres from the group. There is no reaction. They continue to stand immobile, closed eyes, weathered skin. Breathing, but barely. The smell of piss and stale body odour hits me and I cover my nose.

Caelyn creeps closer, until she's less than a metre away from one of them: an old woman with long, grey hair.

I can't bear to watch. There's something so unnatural about these people that I want to be far, far away. 'This is so fucked,' I hiss at her. At any moment their eyes are going to open and they'll come after us like zombies. 'Come on,' I say, 'let's go.

We're in a horror movie and we're the dumbarses who are going to be killed.'

Caelyn shushes me. She inspects the woman in front of her. The woman wears a long, tattered floral dress. Her sunken eyes are closed and her mouth is open, just a little. Her lips are dry and cracked. Her skin is dirty and sunburned.

'Hey,' Caelyn says, but the woman doesn't respond.

Caelyn leans down and picks a long blade of grass. She's about to run it along the woman's face when we hear a voice, and my heart jumps out of my chest.

'Young wanderers,' the man says, 'please leave our seedlings to make the most of Sol's Total Light.'

I look over to see a tall, white, bearded man with shoulder-length hair, overalls and a red plaid shirt. Good-looking, with a broad smile. The sort of man you'd expect might lead a cult of people pretending to be trees.

'Cult leader,' I whisper.

Caelyn ignores me. 'Total light?' she says, dropping the blade of grass and backing away.

He waves at the sky, blue and cloudless.

'Oh,' she says, 'that.'

He says, 'Now, if you could just give our seedlings some space so that their earth and air is less disturbed by your animal exuberances. Come over here.' He beckons. He's polite, but it is an order.

We move toward him.

'Now,' he says, smiling beautifully, 'who are you and what are you doing here?'

Caelyn offers her hand and says, 'Sorry for our ignorance. I'm Caelyn, and this is my partner, Bren.'

The man nods, shakes her hand briefly. 'Ved,' he says.

'I'm writing an article on your organisation,' she says, 'and since I couldn't find a phone number or an email address, I thought I'd visit.'

The man's smile is gone, replaced by a steely frown. 'We aren't an organisation. And we don't have contact details.'

'Right,' she says. 'Which is why I'm here.'

He looks across at me. 'Why are *you* here?'

'I like nature,' I say. The man's expression doesn't change, and I add quickly, 'I'm just here to support her.'

'I'm not writing clickbait,' Caelyn says. 'I'm not looking to shame or discredit anyone.'

'I chased off a few hikers with video cameras a few months ago. We don't need any more gawkers.'

'I'm just interested in what you have to say,' she says. 'What you believe in.'

He studies her face for a long time. Caelyn holds her nerve. 'Stillness,' he says eventually.

'I might need more than that for an article,' she says.

He grins and looks away. 'Okay, okay. Couldn't hurt to get the word out, I suppose. A few conditions though: no names, no video, no recording. No identifiers. If people need to find us, they will. Like you, apparently.'

'Is that how it works?' she asks.

'Do you accept the conditions?'

'I do,' she says.

The warm, generous smile returns to his face. 'Come,' he says, 'you won't find the conversation you seek here. The rest of the hopefuls and caretakers live in a camp not far away. You can join us for lunch.'

'No, thanks,' I say, as Caelyn says, 'Great.'

'Read it to me,' I say, handing her a mug.

Caelyn looks at her laptop and winces. 'Ugh,' she says. 'It's so stupid.'

'I bet it's not. Come on, read it. It'll help.'

She takes a breath and begins. '*In a field beside an old-growth forest, down a long, cracked dirt road* . . . No. Logging road. Just logging road.' She taps on her keyboard.

'Keep going,' I say. 'It's fine.'

'*In a field beside an old-growth forest, down an old logging road, thirty-three people face east and believe they are becoming trees. I don't mean that they wake up and decide to be a tree for the day and then go home. I mean that they have stood in the same place for weeks on end, barely eating, barely drinking, trusting that they will soak up the nutrients provided by the sun, the earth and the air. I stand before them, challenging them, daring them to move, but they don't. Within a few moments a voice asks me to give the seedlings space to bathe in Sol's Total Light for as long as the day will allow. A middle-aged man appears: long hair, beard, plaid shirt; the sort of man you'd expect to meet in a commune dedicated to people pretending to be trees.*'

'Hey,' I say, 'that was my joke.'

'It was a good joke. I'm using it.'

'What if I wanted to write an article?'

'You're not going to write an article. May I continue?'

'Sure.'

'Um . . . *the sort of man you'd expect to meet in a commune dedicated to people pretending to be trees. He calls himself Ved, or Forest Walker. He invites me for lunch in what he calls the Wanderers' Camp. And then things get weirder.*'

'Where am I?' I say.

'You're in the background. Haunting. There's a break here, and then: *They call themselves the Southern Ocean Arborealist Society but refer to themselves more commonly as the Arborealists. Ved tells me they've made camp here for several months. The land itself is in a strange sort of dead zone. Originally Wadawurrung Country, it was for a time owned by a company that was not permitted to log it but did so anyway. Many hectares of old-growth forest were destroyed before the logging was finally stopped by a reluctant state government. The company went bust, its directors absconded, and the land remains trapped in a legal limbo that will take years to resolve. When I ask Ved whether this history had anything to do with why they chose this site, he says that they don't know how they ended up there, they just did.*'

She pauses and looks up at me. 'Is this . . . ?'

'Keep going.'

She continues: '*Ved doesn't say much as we walk down the hill to the camp. At the bottom, a healthy creek flows beside a small collection of tents and makeshift huts. There are a few dozen people here, tending the campfire, stirring pots, talking, eating, reading.*

Only a few glance up when I arrive. I look around for evidence of mistreatment – the possibility that those on the hill are there under duress has occurred to me – but I can't see anything obvious. Ved leads me to the fire and says, 'Let me introduce you to some of the aspirants and the caretakers.'

'I notice you haven't mentioned the smell,' I say.

'Yeah, nah, I thought that would be unkind.'

'*He introduces me first to a woman named Plinth, who has been carving a thick branch. Until recently, Plinth was an English teacher at a top private school.* What are you carving? *I ask. She holds out the piece of wood for my inspection.* It's hard work being a seedling, *she says.* Most need help to stay standing, so we make them little scaffolds. *She makes a few careful cuts.* And before you ask, yes, this is a branch that was fallen. *The way she says it – as if it was descended from heaven.*

'*An older man, who introduces himself as Tol, says that Plinth is a good caretaker.* It sounds like it, *I say. He asks if I have heard the call too. The group quietens for a moment, waiting for my response. I say that I've certainly heard something. He nods, and Ved nods, and apparently that's enough for them.*'

Caelyn scratches her head. 'I don't know,' she says, 'does this even work?'

'It works,' I say. 'Keep reading.'

She screws up her nose, as if disgusted by what she sees on the screen in front of her, but continues.

'*The Arborealists believe in the supremacy of trees over all life, the power of Sol and its Total Light, the sustenance of the Dirt Mother and the life-spreading properties of the Great Current (the wind).*

They divide themselves into three cohorts: aspirants, seedlings and caretakers.

'*The aspirants, who currently number fifteen but are, according to Plinth, increasing in number daily, have arrived hoping to become a seedling. Becoming a seedling, however, is not a simple process.*

'*An aspirant must first prepare. Plinth tells me it takes months of training. They spend their days meditating and exercising. Quieting the mind, readying the body, for the Stilling.* It is a giving of one's animal spirit to the plant, *Ved tells me.* It is the renunciation of muscle and animal consciousness. It is to be in the place where you have landed, to love it and nurture it, to drink from it, to eat from it. It is to give everything and be given everything.

'*The caretakers have usually tried and failed to become trees, and wait for the right time to try again. In the meantime, they look after the seedlings, providing them with water when there's not enough rain, propping them up when their muscles fail to resist gravity and dealing with pests.*

'*The origins of this group are obscure. There is no obvious internet presence. They claim there is no conspiracy, that it is not a cult, and that no-one has organised it through a clandestine forum. And from what I've seen, the usual cult elements – the charismatic but ruthless leader, the manifesto – are not present. They've never advertised or sought new members. It started with Tol and a few of the seedlings. Then a few more showed up. Then more. There was no structure, no order. No-one asked me to become part of the movement. When asked why they came, Ved says,* We were called, and we arrived.

'Called by whom? *I ask him.*

'He shrugs. I press him for more and he gestures at the sky, the earth, the nearby forest. We were called, and we arrived.

'Tol claims that some of the seedlings have been standing there for three months. They appear more malnourished and weaker than the others. I ask the group whether what is happening is humane. Whether the seedlings should be given routine medical inspections and brought to hospital for treatment if necessary. The group reacts badly.

'One of the caretakers, Kerr, calms them. It's fine, *they say*. You don't get it. But ask yourself: how could a doctor treat a human who is becoming a tree? What use is their knowledge of human anatomy?

'*I say*, They are human, though. They stand, they move slightly, their muscles get sore. I heard one of them moaning earlier. They're human, and they're suffering.

'*The group falls silent. Some of them excuse themselves.*

'*Plinth explains*, Taking root is a slow process. *I ask her if any have managed to do so. She looks at me sadly and says*, No. We had a few who were close. But not yet. *She walks off without explaining.*

'*I have so many more questions. What happened to the ones who were close? Did they just go home? Did they get some medical attention? Are they dead? But I'm left with no-one else to ask.*

'*I hike back to the car. As I drive away, I can't stop thinking about the people on the hill, the seedlings, and the families and friends they might've left behind. I wonder why they are all standing there, undoubtedly in intense pain, not speaking, not moving, and not eating and drinking. Why they are all slowly killing themselves. What brings people to this point?*

'*I stop for petrol in a nearby town and ask the attendant if she's heard of the people trying to become trees. She snorts.* Yeah, *she says.* She holds her hands up in mock panic. The trees are coming, the trees are coming!

'*The sun sets as I resume the long drive home. I try to imagine what it would be like. A foot becoming a root. Skin becoming bark, my torso a trunk and my arms branches. It's ridiculous, and I should be laughing about it. But something about their sincerity has shaken me. And left me strangely hopeful.* What if?, *I think, as the sun's Total Light disappears, the Great Current moves onward, and the world fades into shadow.*

'And scene,' she says, bowing slightly in her chair.

I applaud. 'A triumph,' I say. 'Five stars.'

'Really?'

'Yes, really. It's beautifully written. One quibble.'

'Oh?' She raises an eyebrow.

'I was there.'

'I told you. You're haunting it, like a ghost in the background. It reads better without you.'

I look at Henry as if to say, *Can you believe this?*, but he's busy talking to the pigeons that have settled on our balcony.

'Ugh,' she says, throwing her phone on the couch next to her.
'What is it?' I say.

She puts on a deep voice and says, *'We thank you for your submission, but unfortunately, etcetera, etcetera.'* She blows a raspberry at her phone. 'Why would anyone want to read an article about people trying to become trees?'

'I'm not sure the article was the point. I think you wanted something to investigate.'

'No-one reads anymore anyway,' she says, dropping her head to her knees.

'Look, you'll get there. Wherever it is, you'll get there.'

She does a double-take. 'What?'

'I just mean you'll find it. Whatever you're looking for, you'll find it. This is part of finding it. In the sense that you at least now know what you don't want to find.'

'Christ on a bike,' she says. She opens her laptop and spends the afternoon applying for jobs she doesn't want and the evening sketching a leaf.

—

She finds a job at a company in the city that requires her to wear business suits. She says the suits make her feel like she can't breathe. I give her three months.

—

We watch an old episode of one of the *Voidstar* comic adaptations. Unlike Caelyn, I was obsessed with the comics as a kid, but avoided this series. It's rated very poorly, and I don't want to ruin my memory of sitting in my room reading those fantastic stories. But despite everything that we can watch, there's nothing we want to watch, so *The Voidstar Chronicles* it is.

It's a long episode supposedly based on issue thirty-two: *The Reckoning with Form*. In the comic, the story begins with Voidstar, who has taken the aspect of a two-legged creature on a planet that is about to be struck by another. They sit on a cliff with several similar creatures watching the incoming planet grow larger in the sky. The group know what is coming. They all know they will be annihilated. Voidstar listens to the creatures talk quietly about the glories that will be lost, the civilisations that came before, the knowledge that will disappear. Eventually, the other creatures ask why Voidstar is so quiet. For the first and only time in the comics, Voidstar seems uncertain. They shake their head and tell the creatures that there is no noise they could make that could convey their thoughts. 'Yet,' Voidstar says cryptically, 'in all universes, it is only this fight that matters. The void will almost always win, but it is overconfident. Life, on the other hand, is sneaky. Hidden. It turns up where you least expect it. It flourishes where it shouldn't. Life will continue. Yes, entropy and death will win here today. But it hasn't won the war. And you will be remembered, in the signals you have sent out to space, in the atoms you have shed and the energy you have expended. You will not be consumed, you will be transformed. You will find other paths, other ways, other waveforms, other stars, other lives. All is not lost, my friends.' The issue ends with panels of the group watching the planet as it gets closer, and closer, until they can no longer be seen.

The adaptation has turned this contemplative story about the rise and fall of civilisations into a cheap 1980s end-of-the-world dance party. There is little of the original story in there, aside from the incoming planet. I point the flaws out to Caelyn several times. Halfway through she falls asleep on my lap. She's been going to sleep earlier and earlier since joining the company that requires a business suit. When we finally go to bed, she mumbles sleepily, 'All is not lost, my friends.'

—

Caelyn commutes to work, and I get sick of working from home by myself for most of the day. Henry doesn't mind alone time. He probably prefers it. I find a temporary office in a small co-working space above Neko's cafe. It's just until I decide on something more permanent. I've never worked in an office before. I assumed there'd be more conversations, but as none of us work for the same company or do similar jobs or have anything in common, we have little to talk about. It's mostly just people clicking, typing, sighing and rushing to breakout rooms to take calls.

Caelyn's work tires her, but she stays at the company. Three months. Four months. Six. When people ask her how she's going, she says, 'Good. Good.' She constantly asks me for shoulder massages.

—

Dad hands Caelyn a plate and makes his usual joke about how skinny she is. Usually she has an acerbic comeback, but this time she just says, 'Ha, yeah.' Travis makes his usual joke about me eating all the food in our house and suggests I visit his gym. I already go to a gym sometimes, but I don't tell him that because that would just encourage him. Instead I say that they're both being very rude, and they laugh and say they're not.

Travis pours wine and says it's from a valley in the Californian desert and that we should detect notes of rattlesnake and methamphetamine. Mum says, 'Travis,' and he says, 'No, seriously, we'll be hearing cedar notes and perhaps pine nuts in this one. It's got character.' Dad says, 'You mean it's shit that you couldn't sell.' Travis points at his chest in mock offence and says, 'Nothing I sell is shit, Dad.'

We talk about the decline of factories in the neighbourhood, rising interest rates and small dogs. No-one mentions that Dad's usual roast potatoes with rosemary and garlic have no rosemary, no garlic, and have been steamed rather than roasted.

Mum tells us that Miles's mum and dad visited. They seemed good, she says. 'You might want to visit them, Bren. I think they'd appreciate it.' I shrug but don't respond. I can see her disapproving stare in my peripheral vision. 'Miles is definitely dead by now,' Travis says. Travis sometimes forgets that he's human. 'Trav,' I say, 'don't say shit like that.' Dad says, 'Not wrong, though.' Mum puts her hand on Travis's forearm. 'He was a good kid,' she says. I say, 'Wherever he is, if he even is alive, he's twenty-five, same as me. Not a kid anymore. And it was his choice to leave the way he did.' Mum shakes her head. 'It was so cruel, though, Bren.' I say, 'Then why is it up to me to fix it? What good will a visit from me do? He left. He's the problem. Or maybe his parents were the problem. Who knows? He never told me. Never said a word about anything that was going on in his head, in his family, nothing. We were barely friends.' Mum sighs and looks away. Dad says, 'Bren.' Travis widens his eyes and takes a large gulp of wine. Caelyn sips hers and says, 'Should I be hearing the soundtrack to *Arrival* in this, Travis? You know, the film with the enormous squid aliens that don't talk but kind of scream? Because that's what I'm hearing.'

—

We find ourselves on the floor after work, watching old *Voidstar* episodes again. I remind Caelyn the comics were better. She says she never trusted comics. On the screen, Voidstar, in this incarnation a small faceless child, sits in front of a sea dividing two cities on a ringworld that encircles a star. 'This from a woman who braids the hair of plants,' I say. She moves closer and rests her head on my chest. 'It's not hair, it's foliage,' she says, before falling asleep.

—

Today the Queue says that I'm to liaise with someone I've never met.

Anton, I liaise, *what sort of work do you do?* The Queue has given me no context apart from his name.

Anton responds immediately. *I am capable of multiple tasks and I appreciate your interest.*

I wonder, not for the first time, if I will ever really understand the job I'm doing or whether it might be time to get a new one.

—

'One of the people I work with asked how I keep getting jobs,' Caelyn says. 'You know, because I've had so many of them.'

I widen my eyes as if to suggest that I'm surprised by this revelation.

'I didn't know how to answer. I just apply and they give them to me.'

When she doesn't elaborate, I say, 'It's probably your incredible personality.'

She nods seriously. 'That is probably a factor,' she says.

—

Morgan calls me up to say that their mum and dad want us to visit for dinner. I ask her why she's calling me about it and not Caelyn, and Morgan says it's easier this way. I say that I don't think it is, and she says I wouldn't understand.

Caelyn's mum and dad make fajitas from a packet and suggest more times than is coincidental that the wine we brought – Travis's – is 'bold'. Morgan and her new boyfriend, Kes, fondle each other under the table. Brenda sips the wine, grimaces, and says to Caelyn, 'So, how's the job?' Caelyn makes an expression that is remarkably similar to her mother's and says, 'Great, Mum, wonderful, yeah. Yesterday I was in a meeting for six hours and the result was that we needed another meeting.' Peter laughs and says in his softened Polish accent, 'Welcome to the world of work, my little scarlet chicken!' He toasts her, then takes a sip of the wine, frowns, and says, 'Is this local? It's very bold. Very many tannins.'

On the way home I ask Caelyn to turn some music on. When she does, I say, 'Thank you, my scarlet chicken.'

'Oh my fucking god, no,' she says, and turns the music off.

—

After work, Caelyn brings back two bottles of wine from her office – she says they were giving them away. I choose to believe her. A bottle down, she says, 'The world is full of fragments. Atoms universes away from other atoms, and all this space in between.'

'How much wine have you had?' I say.

She pushes my knee with her foot.

'No, listen,' she says. 'Our imagination fills in the gaps, so we build this narrative that gives us the illusion that life has been lived linearly. But it's a bunch of dots on a page. So much of what we remember we have invented.'

—

'A cynic is just a disappointed optimist,' Caelyn says, as we find our seats in the theatre.

'I think I'm just disappointed,' I say.

'No,' she says, pointing to our row, 'deep down you believe in the goodness of people. It's one of the things I admire about you. That and your lovely mouse-brown hair.' She tries to run her hand through my hair but I'm too quick and fend her off.

We sit down and I hand her some popcorn. 'We'll see where I land with humanity after *Catamaran Davey 2 – Archipelago of Sin*.'

She settles into her chair and grins. 'Gonna be great,' she says. She grabs an enormous handful of popcorn and stuffs it into her face.

—

I come home from my temporary office to find Caelyn reading a book next to the window. It's summer, the evening sun is golden and the shafts of light dance around the room, bouncing off floating dust and her dark red hair. She looks up at me and smiles and the light is so bright and warm I can't help myself. I take her in my arms and she squeals, kicking her legs playfully as we go to the bedroom.

Afterward, we lie on our backs, the sun now set and the night sky overwhelmed with city light, the curtain swaying, a car in the street reversing, a warm floral wind brushing our skin in gentle waves. She tells me again that she wants to go back to university. I ask her what she would study. Her hand draws imaginary tattoos on my hip. She says she wants to study plants. I say that she does love plants.

'But more than that,' she says. 'Something more than just plants.'

'Is this an excuse to take mushrooms?'

She laughs lightly through her nose, and we don't say anything for a while. She props herself on an elbow and looks at me. 'I have a feeling, Bren. I've had it ever since we went to that forest. There's something there, I don't know. Something I want to follow to see where it goes.'

'Then you should do it.'

'I wasn't asking for permission.'

'I know.'

'Okay,' she says, lying back down.

'It sounds like a great idea,' I say.

'You think so?' she says, sitting up again.

'I do. That . . . visit . . . and the article you wrote, I think you could do more with it. And you do love plants.'

'It's just that I say this sort of thing a lot.'

'You do.'

'And I worry that I'm doing it again, and I'll move on in a few months.'

'Then that's what happens,' I say.

I wonder to myself whether I'm more agreeable after sex, and if she'd been waiting for this moment to bring it up. But it doesn't matter: she's only asking for my support, and I would give that to her in whatever state I was in, no matter what she asked, no matter where she wanted to go, whether she loved me or didn't.

'I think you're extraordinary, Caelyn. And extraordinary people should do extraordinary things.'

She smiles briefly and lies back down. 'Shut up,' she says.

2

The pub where we meet is near the university, mostly frequented by the sort of student who can afford to drink and academics with a stable job. It's very quiet.

I put three pints of beer on the table.

Arlene says, 'That exam was brutal. I'm so tired.' She looks it. Arlene is the only other student over the age of twenty in their classes. She and Caelyn both feel ancient at twenty-eight.

Caelyn nods. 'Least it's over.' She takes a long drink from her glass. Spring sunshine, filtered by the leaves of the plane tree outside, dances across the table.

Arlene looks at her sharply. 'You barely studied.'

'I studied.'

This is technically true. But it mostly involved watching episodes of *Investigatore Polizia* while scrolling websites. The ease with which she's moved through her degree has been incredible.

'The point is,' she adds, 'we're done.'

'Yeah,' Arlene says. 'Well, I am. If I never look at another cell again it'll be too soon. Meanwhile, you're already teaching first years and you'll be rocketing through your PhD next semester.'

'I still need to come up with a research proposal,' Caelyn says.

Arlene waves dismissively.

'You've got ideas,' I say. 'I thought you had ideas?'

Arlene smiles. 'She's got so many ideas.'

Caelyn looks around the room uncomfortably. 'I find it hard picking just one.'

'You've got a few months,' I say. I hold up my glass for a toast. 'For now, congrats to the two oldest people at the university for finishing degrees they could have finished a decade ago.'

'Fuck you,' they say in unison.

Morgan has a baby and calls her Penny.

We visit her and her occasional partner Kop in the hospital. Kop smiles at us weakly and says he's going to get sandwiches. Morgan looks annoyed at him but beams at us.

Caelyn freezes when she sees the baby lying calmly on her sister's chest.

Morgan says, 'Look who's come to visit, Pen!'

Caelyn is still standing in the doorway, so I usher her forward. It takes some effort, but eventually we move in and sit by the bed.

Morgan's usually spiky aura has softened. She's smiling, for a start. But as I've learned from many years of video games, blunt weapons can do just as much damage as sharp ones.

The red, wrinkled baby doesn't move. We stand in silence until Morgan insists that Caelyn hold her. Caelyn says no, no, and is about to leave again when Morgan shoves the baby into her arms. Caelyn holds her hesitantly, but when the baby makes a sound – not a cry exactly; more an expression of the encounter's awkwardness – Caelyn returns her to her mother.

We chat for a while and make amazed sounds at the appropriate moments. Kop returns and hands us each a salmon sandwich. Morgan says, 'Did they not have tuna?' Kop says they did. Morgan frowns and says, 'Well why the fuck didn't you get me tuna then? You know how I feel about salmon farms.' Kop mumbles that he'll go back and slinks away.

There's another silence before Caelyn gets up and says, 'Right, that's us then – congrats, sis, bye!' She kisses Morgan on the cheek and pokes Penny gently on the shoulder.

—

I eat a baguette at Neko's cafe below my temporary office. Across the road a man paints a mural on the wall of an old photography shop. He carefully creates leaves, stems, trunks and boughs. It looks like he's creating an entire forest.

Neko watches with me for a few moments before going back to the coffee machine. 'He came in yesterday,' he says. 'Strange guy. When I asked him about it, he just said, "The trees are coming." Fucking junkies, man. I called the council and they said it was a permitted street art space.' He comes back to the window. 'Looks good, though.'

I agree.

—

I tell Caelyn about a recurring dream I've been having recently. There's a war, I say, and everyone is on a different side. Anyone you see you must kill. It's a mess of blood and destruction. 'So, me and you are at war?' she asks, pointing a finger gun at my head. I put my hands up. 'You have my unconditional surrender,' I say. 'I don't take prisoners,' she says, and shoots.

What I've learned from Henry is that it's okay to get excited about having a shit.

—

It's raining on the way to our favourite ramen place and we each have an umbrella. Caelyn asks if I remember when she shared her umbrella with me that time. She says she was nervous. I say that I bet I was nervouser. She says that not every moment has to end in a punchline, puts her umbrella down and huddles underneath mine.

A few metres later I say, 'But that wasn't a punchline.'

—

We're at Natalie's for a role-playing game. My character is a ranger who prefers the indoors and Caelyn's is a wizard who doesn't believe she needs to use components to cast spells, and so is always failing at casting spells. Sonny asks about my promotion. I say that I used to work on the Queue and now I curate part of the Queue. Caelyn says, 'You're a Queue Curator now and it's way more than just that.' I wait for her to justify her statement, but Natalie makes Caelyn roll a skill check. It fails, and the small display of fireworks Caelyn was attempting – to impress villagers who may or may not be vampires – dissipates into a sad fart emanating from her finger. Natalie actually makes the sound effect. She's really good at it.

—

While I wait for my morning flat white, Neko says, 'So, what's this new job?'

'Same kind of thing,' I say, 'but now I mostly assign work packages rather than doing them. Sometimes I have to tell people to work faster. Sometimes I have to tell them they're doing a good job. Sometimes I have to find out why I haven't heard from them for several weeks.'

'Sounds shithouse. Hey, you know that tree mural?'

I say that I do. It was finished a few days ago. I still don't know if it's comforting or terrifying.

'Well, you're standing next to the artist.' Neko gestures toward the small man standing next to me.

'Really?' I say, turning to him. 'Great work. It's so lifelike. A bit ominous, if you don't mind me saying.'

The man looks up at me as if I'm not quite there. A few awkward moments pass, but eventually there's a glimmer of recognition, as if he's just noticed me. 'Sure,' he says. 'I mean, thanks.'

'It's like *Where the Wild Things Are*,' I say. 'When the kid's room becomes a forest. Except it's a city becoming a forest. Like it once was, maybe.'

His eyes widen, and he says, 'Soon enough.' He looks troubled for a moment. 'Wait, are you one of . . .' He trails off.

'One of what?' I say.

He shakes his head.

'What's the mural called?' I ask.

'*Arborescens*,' he says. 'They're all called *Arborescens*.'

Neko hands him his coffee. 'There are more of them?' he says.

'Sounds Latin,' I say.

The artist nods and doesn't say any more. I watch as he leaves. His limbs twist strangely and jerk suddenly sometimes, as if they aren't used to movement.

'Fucking junkies,' Neko says after he's gone.

—

At my office I look up *'arborescens'* online and learn that it's Latin for 'becoming a tree'.

At lunchtime I think back to the people we saw standing in a field a few years ago. I wonder what happened to them. I imagine them as rows of fern people, with long ferny beards and arms curled up in a spiral. Becoming trees. I text Caelyn about it and she writes back, *Hmm.*

We spend a two-week holiday in Italy to celebrate Caelyn's graduation. We leave Henry with Mum and Dad. Dad never remembers his name, so calls him 'Peanut'. Henry doesn't seem to mind, and is happier with Mum's attention than he's ever been. Caelyn travels aggressively, like a bird freed from her cage. Every day is something different, every moment a chance to see something we haven't seen before. She takes a billion photos and posts them on social media alongside quotes from poets I haven't heard of.

At a trattoria next to our hotel in Rome, we watch a man walk into the middle of the street and refuse to move. Cars swerve out of his way, but he doesn't shift. Eventually police arrive and try to convince him to leave. He doesn't respond. They attempt to physically pick him up, but he's too heavy or they don't care that much. I have several serves of gelato and declare it the best thing I've ever eaten. Caelyn says absently that it's not the food I'm eating, it's something else. She waves mystically at the buildings around us and the ancient vine-covered aqueduct that towers above. She puts her pen down, sighs, and rests her head on my shoulder. 'I wish this was life,' she says.

'How so?' I say.

'This movement,' she says, 'this newness, these buildings, this man standing in the street, everything. I wish I was on a train whose tracks encircled the globe, getting off for a few days every now and then but always moving. Seeing something new every day.'

'That'd be nice,' I say. 'But wouldn't you want a place to come home to?'

'That's the thing,' she says, 'the train would be home. It'd have rooms and furniture and books and all that. It'd just be moving.'

Later, we go to a bar and meet Arlene, who has decamped to Rome for the foreseeable future and is now an expert on everything Roman. She speaks in an exaggerated Italian accent when she orders food. We drink a few bottles of wine and stumble back to our hotel where, in the road, the man still stands, surrounded by witches' hats.

—

At 3 am Caelyn sits up in bed and says, 'The tree people,' then falls back to sleep.

She frequently sits up in bed at 3 am and says things like, 'Gremlins on the roof,' or, 'Grass babies in her ears,' so I don't think anything of it.

—

One night in the hotel room, she watches a video of people in Amsterdam standing next to a canal. Cyclists yell at them to get out of the way. One person throws a plastic bottle at them.

No-one in the group moves. After a few minutes of this, someone pushes one of them into the water. At first people laugh. The camera operator, who has been making insightful commentary like, 'Oh, man,' and, 'What the fuck?' laughs too. But when the woman hits the water she doesn't flail, she sinks. Laughter turns to panic, and someone from a passing boat jumps in and rescues her. The video ends with a close-up of the woman's face as she lies on the deck of the boat. It is expressionless, unmoving. It's difficult to say whether she's alive or not. Caelyn shows me this without a word, gets up and looks out the window. She says that the man on the street is still standing there.

—

We go on a tour to an ancient olive grove in Puglia, its gnarled, centuries-old trees still being harvested for olive oil. On a long table, under the branches of one of the oldest trees, lunch is laid out for us. The tour guide says the tree is old enough to have seen the Roman Empire rise and fall. I eat and drink, then alarm a retired American couple by exaggerating the deadliness of Australian spiders. Caelyn ignores the food and the group, and sits against the trunk of another tree, writing and sketching.

—

Her notebook is covered with drawings of leaves and bark and vines and people pretending to be umbrella pines and cypresses.

—

We spend our last evening in Italy back in Rome, at the same hotel. The man on the street is no longer there. Caelyn asks the manager of the hotel what happened to him.

The manager shrugs. 'They removed him. They needed many workers. They said he was stuck like a fat man.' He laughs. 'But you saw him. This was not a large man.'

—

'Something's happening,' she says. 'You can feel it, can't you? The guy in the street, those people in the video. Doesn't it look connected to the people we saw at home a few years ago?'

'Just looks like a bunch of people standing around. Bit of a difference.'

She shakes her head. 'The manager said the guy was stuck.'

'Probably glued his shoes to the asphalt.'

'There's something happening,' she says again.

On the tarmac the airplane inches closer to the runway, and pretty soon we're roaring through the atmosphere. She doesn't sleep the entire way home. Instead, she types and reads and types some more. Somewhere over Malaysia, she tells me she knows what she has to do, and I say fine and fall back to sleep wondering whether we'll be getting breakfast or dinner next, and what sort of alcohol works with breakfast.

—

'Wait,' I say, bleary-eyed from sleeplessness and poorly timed whisky, 'you said you know what you have to do. What does that mean?'

The baggage claim is stuffed with people who all believe their bag will be the next to arrive.

Her lack of sleep is beginning to catch up with her too. She waves me away. 'Later,' she says, yawning. 'Much later.'

The guy who usually cuts my hair no longer cuts my hair and it's freaking me out because I can no longer be sure of what's going to happen when I go there.

—

Dad hands me a beer and says that he's fed up with the rule changes. I nod and watch as a player I don't know kicks the ball for what I assume is a goal but isn't. 'Why isn't that a goal?' I ask Dad. 'Ah,' he says, waving at the television, 'corrupt bastards.' Outside I see Mum on the back deck, drinking gin in what little sun is left. 'Should she be drinking?' I ask Dad. 'Isn't she on stuff?' Dad looks at her through the window. As always, his gaze lightens when it lands on her. I don't know how they've been in love for so long. 'You going to stop her?' he says. He turns back to the television. 'Now, who do we have here?'

—

There are too many ways we can pretend we're not here.

—

My co-worker, whose name is Ally, asks what my relationship with my brother is like. I've never had an interaction with Ally that isn't confusing. I ask how they know about Travis.

It's on your profile, they message.

No it's not, I reply.

Not yours, another person's.

Right, I type. I don't feel comfortable talking about this with a co-worker I've never met in person.

This is a safe space, Bren.

Yeah, look, I just want to find out about the status of that work package.

Hey, have you heard about formesteen?

It's weird how you keep sending me links to strange shit I've never heard of without context, Ally. I'm not going to click your links.

I thought this was a safe space, Bren.

I would like to ask Ally if they are real or another advanced, self-replicating simulation, but it's against the company's People Policy, so I don't. I would like it if I could do a job that paid well and let me hold something real in my hands for a while, but that's not the way the current wave of capitalism works, whatever it's called.

—

'I'm going to do my PhD in psychobotany and conceptions of human–plant hybridity,' Caelyn announces to her family.

Morgan, Penny, Morgan's new partner Kreg (who looks unsure if he should be here), Brenda and Peter all fall silent.

Her family cultivate long silences. There are at least three every time they meet. They revel in it. I don't, so I jump in. 'You got accepted?'

She nods. 'Yep. Not sure about the supervisor, but whatever.'

Brenda says, 'You're going to be, what, a plant expert?'

Caelyn shovels in a dumpling and says between chews, 'Something like that.'

Morgan laughs. 'You kill every plant you buy,' she says.

Caelyn's eyebrows twitch slightly, then she smiles. 'Well,' she says, 'maybe I'll be able to keep them alive now. And I'm not – it's not about looking after plants. I'll be looking at how people have conceived of humans as trees, both now and in the past. Did you know there's an old Welsh poem from the Middle Ages about an army of trees?'

Peter changes the subject to the football and everyone seems happier.

As we're leaving, Peter pulls Caelyn aside and says that he's proud of her. She hugs him tightly. She hugs her mother and her sister and they all hug me. Kreg, who's only been on the scene for a few weeks as far as I know, waves. He's not in hugging territory yet and he knows it. I give him a thumbs up for encouragement.

I drive away. Caelyn stares out at the passing world. She says, 'I thought they'd understand.'

I glance over at her.

'I thought Morgan would,' she continues. 'You know how we grew up next to that little forest? We were always there, just the two of us, exploring, making up games. It was magical. And then Mum got a job at the uni and we had to move to the city. I don't think I've ever gotten over it. Maybe Morgan wasn't as happy in the country as I was. And I really thought Mum would be pleased that I'm following in her footsteps. Dad doesn't mind what I do. I just thought he'd be more . . . I don't know. I assumed they'd all think this was a good idea.'

Halfway between her parents' house and home, in the long-shadowed space between suburbs, she says, quietly, 'This PhD is important, Bren. Not just for me personally. There's something bigger.'

I say that I'm with her, and she says she knows, and wraps her arm around mine.

—

When I return home from work the next day, Caelyn has drawn flowers and leaves all over my desk with permanent marker. I tell her it's an act of vandalism, and she says it's a shit desk and, if anything, it's worth more now. I tell her that's not the point, but while she waits for me to explain the point, I realise I don't know what it is, so I just say, 'Thank you for my new desk.'

Another drone flies past on whatever obscure business it's on. I stick my finger up at it. Travis throws me the basketball and says he's heard that, in some companies, alternative intelligences have hired human actors to play them at social events. Within a few seconds he steals the ball from me and scores. He's always been my physical superior and not averse to demonstrating it. I accept this and bide my time until I can devastate him at our annual family trivia competitions.

I ask him what companies, and he says it's true, they can simulate human faces in online meetings, but when it's time to show up for an event in person, it's more complicated.

He throws me the ball again and says, 'Because, you know, bots are employees now. With salaries and everything. But even though they're exempt from going to social events because they aren't physical entities, they believe that social events are how humans get ahead in the workplace. And so there's this whole black market of people being paid to be a real-life avatar of AI. All these out-of-work actors with earpieces doing whatever these bots tell them. It's fucked up, man.'

'Have you actually seen this happen?'

I sit down on the side of the court. Travis does a few more lay-ups. He always likes to prove that he has more left in the tank.

'Don't need to see something to know it's happening,' he says, adding, 'swish,' as the basketball falls cleanly through the hoop. Doesn't know where Paraguay is, though.

—

'Hey,' Lee says, 'what if everyone in this pub is an actor pretending to be someone they're not?' Out the window, a driverless car attempts to park in a space nearby that is clearly too small for it.

'Christ,' I say, 'what have you and Travis been reading?' The driverless car is persistent and doesn't seem to mind the line of traffic that's forming behind it.

'Reading?' Lee says.

I don't know how to respond to that, so I ask about his kids, who are the last people I want to know about.

—

'Does it ever occur to you that these shows are designed to appeal to us according to an elaborate set of psychological and psychosocial principles that have been endlessly studied and fed into machines to produce content that is different enough to appear novel but somehow is all exactly the same?' I say.

Caelyn says, 'Mm-hmm,' and concentrates on the young man who has lost his family to a marauding pack of mercenaries and has encountered an old hermit who was once a grand sword master but had grown jaded. 'The difference,' she says, 'is that this one is set in the seventh century.'

'But they're all full of the same story beats that elicit specific emotional reactions at the same time,' I say. 'We're being manipulated. We're being programmed. Controlled by algorithms.'

'I've been warning you about the robots,' she says.

'The correct term is alternative intelligences. Oh look, he's going to train.'

Caelyn shushes me. She loves training montages.

—

'There's nothing dystopian about any of this,' the man in the carriage says to his companion. 'I mean, I'm still drinking coffee.' He holds up his cup. The other man says, 'I'm not sure the dystopian index is centred around the availability of coffee, mate.' The coffee-holding man says, 'Wrong, mate, the day we run out of coffee is the day we've officially landed in a dystopia. Fucking zombies will be everywhere.' They both laugh as though everyone on the train should know how funny they are.

—

I collect lemons in a bucket from the tree at Mum and Dad's house.

Dad puts a few lemons in the bucket. 'Another lemon tart for Caelyn?' he says.

'No,' I say, 'I'm doing some preserving.'

'She loves lemon tarts,' he says.

'No, *I* like lemon tarts. Caelyn goes to great lengths to ensure there are no lemon tarts on the menu in any cafe we go to because she can't stand them.'

'Bit of ice cream,' he says, 'just to smooth it out, nothing better. Your mother makes the best lemon tarts. Don't blame Caelyn for loving them.' He reaches for another lemon. 'When's your mother going to make it? Wouldn't mind some myself.'

'I'm making it, Dad,' I say, then shake my head. 'No, hang on, I mean I'm preserving the lemons. I'm not making a lemon tart. Mum never made lemon tarts anyway.'

'Down at the store,' he says.

'Right, no-one ever made lemon tarts in this family. It was all store-bought.'

'Right,' he says. He hands me a few more lemons. 'Phew. What are you going to do with these lemons?'

'I'm going to preserve them, Dad,' I say.

—

The Queue keeps growing, no matter how many work packages we process. People keep getting added to my team to keep up with the demand. My manager, Bowden, usually tells me I'm doing a good job but never gives me any proof.

I often daydream about sitting in the shade of a palm tree next to a beach with white sand. But whenever I've visited these kinds of places, I've felt incredibly uncomfortable. The sand is too gritty, the beach is too steep, the water is murky or rough, there are sharks, whatever. But my dreaming mind thinks this place is out there and the ones I've actually visited are poor imitations. I don't know what my brain wants.

—

She talks endlessly about trees. She often stays at the university long into the evenings. Our bookcases heave with botanical art and scientific textbooks on the nature of stamens or bark, and old pictures of people who appear to be trees or trees who appear to be people. She reads medieval texts about armies of trees, about a baron who ruled his realm from the boughs, about trees that are not trees but the hands of giants buried deep in the ground. She has found it, that thing that she wanted to find. She fills notepads with intricate drawings of petals and leaves and wood. She writes and writes. She is joyful and stressed, often at the same time. She's going to do more teaching, she says, but I'm worried about money, and I'm worried that I haven't found my thing, and I'm worried that I should be happier for her, and I'm worried that, as a heterosexual male partner of a heterosexual woman in the first half of the twenty-first century, I should be able to support her dream and forgo dreams of my own, but something about that remains hard to swallow – you could call it the patriarchy still clawing at me – even if I have no great dreams of my own, and can't find dreams of my own no matter how hard I look; it's just the idea that, if I did have dreams of my own, I wouldn't be able to follow them now because she takes up all the air; and I'm worried that I'm selfish to make this about me, I'm antiquated, I'm a sad and defeated misogynist; but I'm still worried.

'Those really are beautiful drawings,' I tell her, and I mean it. 'Like, I'd get a tattoo of that tree.'

She beams a little but downplays it and says, 'They aren't really that good.' I say they are, and she says, 'It's an apple tree.' I ask if she wants some lemon tart, and she screws up her nose and says, 'We've talked about this.'

Caelyn says she's going to interview the tree people we met a few years ago for her thesis. I tell her that I don't think we should go back there, and she says, 'Who said anything about "we"?' She likes to remind me sometimes she can do fine by herself.

I say that I'm pretty sure it was a murder cult.

'Fuck off,' she says. 'They weren't murderers. They were people trying to find their way. Trying to find their way back to the earth. That's it.'

'You don't deny the cult bit, though,' I say.

She clenches her teeth. She says, 'I just need to check in on them, do some interviews and then leave. You can take some photos if you like. That'd be helpful.'

—

We arrive at the car park down the dirt road, just as we did years ago. We get out and breathe in the air.

Caelyn looks confused. 'Something's different,' she says.

I take a few deep breaths. 'It is,' I say.

We are still surrounded by tall mountain ash, and the forest floor is still covered with large tree ferns. But there is a disturbance in the air, a slowing of time.

We take our packs and walk. Caelyn looks up at the canopy repeatedly. A few minutes down the track, she takes my elbow. 'It doesn't feel right,' she says.

I nod. It doesn't feel as oppressive as it did the last time.

Her gaze is fixed on the trees, so I lead her along the path, warning her of uneven ground, rocks and roots.

We come to the creek where she once pounced on me. 'Do you remember what you did here?' I ask.

Her face has lost its colour.

'You pretended I was a deer or something coming down to a waterhole, and you were like a jaguar.'

Her gaze doesn't leave the trees as she says, 'I was a cougar.'

I release her arm and splash water on my face. It's cold and it stings.

'There aren't any birds,' she says. 'I can't hear any birds.'

She's right. There's more light peeking through the canopy. And it is so quiet. No birds, no scurrying mammals or reptiles, no insects. Not even any flies.

'It shouldn't be this peaceful,' Caelyn says.

I say that I like it. 'Thought the forest was going to eat me last time.'

'Not the time for jokes Bren.'

A few years ago she knew nothing about any of this. She's suddenly an expert in everything botanical, in everything green and environmental, but I'm still the one keeping the plants in our apartment alive. She takes a few steps off the trail to greet an enormous tree trunk. Running her hands over the bark, she murmurs something. She sits down in the decaying old roots and rests the back of her head on the tree.

I whisper, 'Are you talking to it?'

She doesn't respond.

'What's it saying? Does it like us?'

She holds her finger up to her lips and breathes in deeply.

We stay there for a while, breathing, listening. The thought crosses my mind that I am unnecessary here, and that my presence may be doing more harm than good.

'Bren,' she says quietly.

'Mmm?' I reply.

She opens her eyes and looks at me. 'Silence is death,' she says.

Her expression darkens and she stands and rushes along the path, soon outpacing me. I'm pretty sure it's not to sneak up on me this time. I lose her in the trees for a while. Every now and then I look behind me, just to make sure there's no red-haired panther about to attack me, but she's never there. I walk slowly. I haven't been exercising as much as I should. We still have about an hour of walking in front of us before we get to the home of the tree people, or whatever they called themselves.

I'm about to look up formesteen on my phone when, far too soon, the canopy breaks, and there is light. I'm at the forest's edge already. The ground is blasted, dead, filled with tracks of logging equipment and hundreds, perhaps thousands, of stumps: blackened, clear-felled, beyond life, beyond healing, gone.

Caelyn sits on the bones of a thick stump. I can see its ghost, eighty metres tall, watching over us; the ghosts of its neighbours, too, and the ghosts of the tree ferns and the brush and the young saplings waiting for their window; the animals and the birds and the insects buzzing, flitting, hiding and hunting and nesting. It's so quiet. She looks out over the devastation. I put my pack down and sit next to her. She doesn't say anything.

'This is fucked,' I say.

'This was old growth. All of this. Fucking centuries. They aren't supposed to do this.'

I say, 'Houses need building, I guess.'

'Fucking houses,' she spits. 'What the fuck is wrong with us, Bren? Why can't we just stop? We know we're killing the planet, we've seen we're killing the planet, and yet we can't stop. We're addicts. You and me too. We're no better. Fucking pigs. Worse than pigs. Pigs are great. And pigs stop eating eventually. We keep going. Eating everything. Leaving nothing. We fucking deserve whatever hell we make.' She pats the stump we're sitting on. 'This was probably three centuries old, and it's not even the biggest one here. Now it's some cunt's rustic dinner table. What the fuck.' She stands and screams. '*What the fuck! Fuck!*' She rubs her head and sits back down. 'You saw the rest of the forest, didn't you? How it knew? It fucking knew. The trees know what happened here.'

I hold up my hand in protest. 'I know you're going to be a doctor soon but that might be a stretch.'

She pokes me in the chest with her finger. 'You said it too. You know it. Don't tell me you don't.'

'Yes, fine, whatever; this is bad, but the government –'

'Oh, fuck the government. I'm so tired of all this. I wish the bastards who did this would turn into trees.' She leans back on the stump, then immediately sits up again. 'Fuck,' she says. She stands, grabs her pack and heads off.

I grab my pack too and stumble after her.

'What?' I say, breathing hard.

She rushes on at a pace I don't match.

—

'There's no-one here,' Caelyn says an hour later. I put my pack down and scan the area. It feels like the same place, but it's hard to tell with the forest gone.

'Are you sure this is it?' I say.

'I think so. Look over there.'

She hurries toward a few dozen stumps, lined up in a row. I continue scanning the horizon for life. She inspects the stumps then waves me over.

'These trees have been cut down,' she says.

'Yes,' I say, 'that's pretty clear. Did you not notice the rest of them?' I take a few photos of the stumps.

'Don't you see what that means?'

'No.' I take off my pack and sit on the grass. It's been a long walk.

'These trees weren't here last time. And they were obviously planted. It's a straight line.'

'So the people who were standing here got bored or died or whatever, and whoever was left planted these trees in their place and left. And then loggers came and cut it all down.'

'No, look,' she says, touching one of the stumps. 'You're not looking. Take this stump. It's, I don't know, twenty years old. But this one is more like fifty or sixty. They were completely different ages, Bren.'

—

At the old camp by the creek, there is ruin. Tents have been scattered and abandoned. The remnants of a bonfire lie in the centre. Melted plastic and charred wood are mixed with metal and rubbish. There's a stink that causes us to hold our nose. I'm not sure if it's death or something else. There's no-one here.

'This isn't good,' I say.

'We should probably leave,' Caelyn says. 'Give me the camera, I just need to get a few specific images.'

I hand her the camera. While she shoots, I poke the fire with a stick. A mixture of ash and mud, scorched earth and unrecognisable objects. 'We're in deliverance territory here,' I say.

'What does that mean?' she says.

'Dad used to say it when we went on fishing trips in the middle of nowhere. I'll look it up.' I take out my phone.

'You don't need to look it up.'

Oh, but I do. I refuse to let trivia like that stay unknown for long. 'It's an old movie,' I say. 'About some crazy country people.'

'Bren,' she says, 'I think they were real.'

'What was real?'

'The trees.'

'Well,' I say, 'yes, they were trees. But if you're implying they were anything else I –'

'I am,' she says firmly, handing the camera back to me. 'I think they were people and some of them became trees. All the evidence I'm seeing –'

I hear the sound of boots crunching on the dry grass nearby. She stops talking. I turn.

'Who are you?' a man says.

I don't respond, mostly because I'm too startled by the branches, leaves and lichens that adorn his body, attached with a mixture of wires, vines, tape and possibly glue.

'Uh,' I manage.

Caelyn puts a palm on my back and gently pushes me forward.

'I'm Bren,' I say, 'and this is Caelyn.'

The man shakes his head angrily. Some plant matter comes loose, but he doesn't seem to notice or care.

'I don't mean your names,' he says. 'What are you doing here?'

'That's not what you asked,' I say.

He frowns. More leaves fall to the ground. Whatever adhesives he's used don't hold up under scrutiny. 'Haven't you fuckers done enough?' he says. 'When they screamed, did you even hear them? What kind of monsters *are* you?'

He takes a step closer and we take a step back.

'Hold on,' I say, 'we're not here to hurt anything. We're here to talk to the people who were here before.'

'There's no-one here anymore,' he growls, 'because you bastards cut them down.'

He advances further. We retreat further.

'Ved,' Caelyn says at last. 'You're Ved. We talked to you a few years ago. You showed us around the camp. I was writing an article about your . . . movement. And you introduced us to Plinth and a few other . . . what did you call them? Saplings?'

He stops and cocks his head, bird-like. A stricken look comes over his face and his body relaxes. More detritus falls. 'Seedlings,' he says. 'They were just seedlings then.'

'We're just here to talk,' I say. 'Caelyn is interested in your ideas. She's doing academic work in, you know, like, trees and people and things.'

'Psychobotany,' she says. 'Specifically around plant–animal metamorphosis states. Your camp and your seedlings, they were – they were beautiful. I'm so sorry about what happened here. I didn't know. I'd love to talk to you about it. I'd love to tell the story. If you'll let me.'

He stares at her a few moments longer than is comfortable.

He sighs and says, 'Yes. I remember you. Okay.' He sits on a nearby rock and gestures for us to take a seat. We sit on the ground facing him. 'Everyone's gone. Most of them had just grown. A few of them didn't make it, but most of them did. There was a row of them up there: some eucalypts, some birch, some beech, all family. The old ones became older. We didn't expect that. We thought they'd all become trees of the same age. But the older the person, the older the tree. It happened over a few days. A few magical, magical days of bark and skin and light. We had a ceremony for them after Plinth took shape.

It was a wonderful evening. We drank and ate and danced. And a few weeks later, the logging trucks came and they destroyed the camp and cut them all down.'

'They cut down people?' Caelyn says, horrified.

'No,' he says. 'They weren't people anymore. *Ow.*' He winces and removes a stick from his hair. 'They cut down trees. So what do you want to know?'

—

We return to the straight row of stumps.

'Where'd they all go, anyway?' I ask.

'They're here,' he says, pointing at the ground.

'No,' I say, 'I know that they're "here", like, spiritually or whatever, but where did they actually go?'

Caelyn says, 'He's saying they're still here.'

Ved points out the stones laid at the base of each stump. Names are scratched into them, as well as a date. 'The date is when they first took root.' He smiles and points to a thick old oak stump. 'That was Marjorie. Youngest eighty-year-old I ever met.'

Caelyn says, 'When we visited they were standing still. Some of them had been here for a few months, but no-one looked like a tree. So how long did it take?'

He shrugs and the branches and leaves left on his body rustle. 'At first a long time. Then, not so long. A few days after they grew roots.' I wonder how much maintenance his branch costume needs.

'Did any of them give up or die?' Caelyn says.

He looks at the ground. 'Yeah,' he says sadly. 'Some stopped and became caretakers. They were too twitchy. Something about their bodies, like they didn't really want to stay still. Like they didn't really believe. You have to believe or it's not going to happen. Most kept at it, though. A couple did die, unfortunately. Their bodies couldn't cope. Something was holding them back. They passed away without any sign of transformation.'

'Jesus,' I say.

'The ones who died – we pleaded with them to give up. To go back to being caretakers for a while. But they refused; wouldn't move, wouldn't eat. They weren't ready, though. Not all of us are ready.'

'What about you?' Caelyn says.

'I'm not ready either,' he says quietly.

Caelyn turns to me and says, 'I'd like to interview Ved. If that okay's with you, Ved?'

He shrugs and sits on Marjorie. 'Fire away,' he says through mossy teeth.

—

'Can you actually believe any of that?' I say as we drive away.

She shrugs. 'I think I do,' she says dreamily. 'I think I know nothing at all. Isn't it wonderful?'

The windows in the car are down and her hair is flying around chaotically as she drives. She stares at the horizon as if she's been waiting for the opportunity to run toward it.

3

Mum and I visit Dad together on his birthday. He's in a nursing home and hasn't remembered my name for a year. When we arrive, he smiles and says, 'Hello, darlings.' He looks at Mum as if sunlight has entered the room – even though he may no longer be sure why. Mum kisses him and he rubs my head vigorously. 'Quite a haircut, champ,' he says.

I tell him about the football and he talks about a game he saw that never took place. It's a confused monologue of goals, mud, elbows to the face, roaring crowds and a team that doesn't exist. I think he's just relaying a few of the thousands of disconnected images related to football that still flood his mind.

Mum holds his hand and listens. She looks tired, but then she's been tired for as long as I can remember. When he finally moved into the home, she cried all the way there. But Dad moved in with barely a complaint. In his first moment of lucidity for some time he said, 'Darl, you need rest.' Of course that made Mum cry more.

We stay for an hour, listening to fragments of invented football anecdotes. I turn the television on to the station that airs football replays twenty-four hours a day. Dad settles back in bed and falls asleep to the sound of a commentator from forty years ago complaining about fancy footwork.

—

'All these old love songs,' Caelyn says, 'put the onus on the listener to save the singer. Like this one.' She starts singing off-key, '*I'd go mad if you weren't with me, you're the only one for me, my little cherub, I'll float out to sea or whatever if you don't love meeee.*'

I notice some people at a table nearby listening and shrink into my seat. She is a terrible singer.

'You know,' she says, 'that kind of shit. If you didn't love me, I'd be fine. Sad probably. But go if you need to, buddy.'

'*Buddy?*' I say.

'We should want each other but not need each other.'

'Please don't sing.'

'I'm a great singer,' she says.

I drain my coffee cup and change the subject. 'More visits next week?'

She's just returned from a visit to another tree community, where three or four people stood in a field pretending to be trees. They're rare and hard to find, but Caelyn has uncovered a few during her research. It's becoming clear that they don't have a unifying belief system and they aren't really cults – they're mostly just people who want to be trees. Her PhD is nearly complete, but she keeps gathering data. For her postdoc, she says. I don't really know what a postdoc is, but I go along with it.

She nods. 'Yeah,' she says, 'even though Gary is adamant that there's no academic value in pandering to the ideas of these "fantasists". Should have asked for a change of supervisor at the start.'

'Well, hopefully you'll be able to get some proof this time.'

She looks up sharply. 'I've told you that there is something in this. I would appreciate some support.'

'At no point have you not had my support.'

'But you don't believe me.'

'I think *you* believe but others need to see evidence.'

'Do you see crows die?' she says.

'What?'

'Have you ever seen a crow die?'

'No, I have never seen a crow die.'

'But they do, don't they? They just find places to go. Private, peaceful places, away from noise and people and other creatures.'

'I just think that you should stick with what you know – that there are a bunch of people trying to become trees – and centre your thesis around that. Believing in their claims and writing about them without evidence makes you seem . . . I dunno.'

She raises her eyebrows. 'Back to what I was saying about love songs.'

I stand up. 'I'll go pay.'

—

At uni, the week after I turned up to class with a sunflower and the lecturer pointed it out to everyone, I was invited to a party. I didn't want to go. I was pretty sure people were going to talk about the sunflower. But I went, and got there early. Caelyn arrived a few minutes later. I recognised her from class, but didn't know her. Her hair was short and ruby bright. The way the room turned, the way my heart started racing. Her limbs swam effortlessly through space, flowing like the long sheer curtains whatever-their-name-was had installed in that shithole of an inner-city share house, flowing and dancing gently in the dry summer breeze. It had been a forty-degree day and the bags of ice in the laundry sink lost their structural integrity almost immediately. She was bristling with anxiety, she told me later. She didn't want to go, but Natalie had insisted, had said she'd regret it or she'd make her regret it, I can't remember which. So Caelyn went and moved the way she did, I told her a joke I can't remember and she laughed, and Natalie drank too much vodka and cranberry, threw up in the sink and screamed at everyone. No-one mentioned the sunflower at all.

—

Sometimes she gives me the same feeling I get when I'm watching certain scenes in a David Lynch movie, those scenes where there's this rising noise and the characters we're following have these awful realisations about something so uncanny, so otherworldly and horrifying, that I can barely look. She smiles a certain way and all I can see is a great void looming, yawning, knocking, just around the corner. I haven't told her this.

—

She revises academic papers on the table while I watch television with the sound down and the subtitles on. 'Is ours a love story, do you think?' she says.

'What else would it be?' I say.

'I don't know,' she says, standing. She grabs an imaginary knife from an imaginary drawer, jumps on top of me and holds the knife to my throat. I laugh as she brings the blade closer to my neck, closer, staring at me with an alarmingly good impression of pure rage. 'A murder mystery,' she says.

'That's a long murder mystery,' I say. 'Anyway, what's the motive?'

She drops the knife and sits back. 'Or maybe,' she says, 'it's a tragedy.' She clutches her throat and falls back on the couch, dead.

I move her legs off mine and stand. 'Oh well,' I say, 'if it's a tragedy, it can wait until after dinner. I'm starving. Hungry?'

Henry appears in the doorway, but Caelyn doesn't answer.

I make dinner and serve it in two bowls. I turn the television up, and as I eat, I watch a show about cat hunters. As in hunters who are cats, not people who hunt cats. I don't want Henry to get the wrong idea about me.

Caelyn lies on the couch the entire time, dead. Henry walks over and settles on her back, but she doesn't move.

When I go to bed two hours later, she comes in and demands to know why I didn't call an ambulance, and I shrug and say maybe it was a murder mystery all along. She says, 'Hmph,' and warms up her dinner in the microwave.

On my way to my temporary office, one of the drones that constantly fly overhead descends and hovers in front of me, blocking my path. I sidestep it and it moves with me. I step back. It follows. I walk into the gutter to go around. It accompanies me. I cross the street. It crosses the street. I duck into a laneway. It does too, but faster. Eventually, it ascends and darts off.

When I get to work, I message my team to apologise for being late. *I was accosted by a rogue drone*, I say. Carmichael says it was probably controlled by a glitching gestalt consciousness. Pina says that gestalt entities don't glitch. Anton says that it was within appropriate behavioural parameters of human–AI interaction. I say, *If you wanted to find out more about me, you could have just asked.* Anton says, *I am unclear on an acceptable response to this anecdotal event.* I say, *Let's just get back to it then.*

—

It's tense at Morgan's house. There's no obvious reason for it beyond the usual. Penny, who is now five and my favourite member of their family aside from Caelyn, stands like a tree in the backyard all afternoon. Usually ravenous, she refuses all food and Morgan's increasingly insistent requests that she eat. Brenda takes out her much-loved shortbread and holds it under Penny's nose, but she refuses to budge. Caelyn says, loud enough that Penny will hear, 'It's probably permanent.' A smile flashes briefly across Penny's face.

'Don't indulge her,' Brenda says.

'This is exactly how it begins, Mum,' Caelyn says. 'We just need to accept it. She's going to be a grevillea soon.'

'No!' Penny shouts. 'A Christmas tree!'

Morgan smiles for the first time all day. Peter demands to know what sort of Christmas tree exactly: a pine tree, a fir tree, or something plastic with sparkly things?

'A Nova Scotian white spruce!' she screams, and proceeds to explain why Nova Scotia sends a Christmas tree to Boston every year, and that Hans Christian Anderson's *The Fir Tree* was a true story.

—

'Morgan's had a tough time,' Caelyn says on the way home.

—

At my temporary office I attempt to find some shape in the Queue, some sense of order, some indication that there is something to latch on to, something real. A purpose for what I've been doing these past few years. It's impossible to find. I'm starting to suspect that the Queue is an experiment, but I don't have proof.

Travis calls, and I know even before he speaks.

'Bren,' he murmurs.

Dad has been a ghost haunting a failing body for years, unaware of why he was trapped there but knowing that he was trapped. A ghost calling through the ether, confused, wandering in the dark; nothing like the real person. For a while there would be an occasional line or word, a flash of recognition: 'New shirt, mate?' or, 'I've still got that postcard you sent me from Avignon,' or, 'Is your mother here or she out with the girls again?' Now, he doesn't speak. His decline has accelerated in the last three months. He doesn't understand language, looks incredibly frail and stares into space. The doctors have been saying he doesn't have long left.

I take a breath. An eternal moment passes. 'When?' I say.

'This morning,' he says. 'Couple of hours ago.'

'Where are you? Where's Mum?'

'At home. Their home.'

'I'll be there soon.'

'Mum says he wanted to be buried under a tree. Did you know about that?'

'I'm on my way, Trav.' I close my laptop and unplug it.

'I don't know how we're going to do that. I don't know, Bren. I'm not sure.'

'I'll be there in twenty.'

—

By the time I arrive, they've taken him away. Mum doesn't cry but doesn't speak either. Travis wonders what sort of wine he should provide for the wake. I tell him one that's alive. He agrees and suggests a spicy riesling. I wander our old family home, expecting Dad to appear in a doorway, or to come in from the garden in his floppy hat, sweating, complaining about the mower.

—

The funeral is in a forest cemetery that I hadn't known existed. It's attended by over a hundred people. I had no idea Dad was loved – or even known – by so many.

'He was a good man,' says Mum, as we wait for the service to begin.

'I know,' I say, 'but. It's a lot of people.'

Travis holds a bottle of riesling.

We bury Dad's ashes in the ground and plant a blue gum seedling over them. I see, over time, his bones becoming bark, his smile embedded in knots and whorls, his essence in its wounds, the twist of his broken old spine in its gnarled trunk. I say a few words, but not many. We stand silently while one of his favourite songs, Leonard Cohen's 'Hallelujah', is played over the speakers. Caelyn puts her hand on my knee, palm up, offering it. I take it, and she squeezes, hard.

Around us, on a hill that overlooks the seaside city I was born in and never really left, the secret chord plays to the quiet audience. Nearby is a row of trees with plaques next to them naming their human partners in rot and renewal. Their branches bend softly in a gentle breeze. There are eucalypts, mostly, but also oaks, cypresses, myrtles, she-oaks, elms and maples. There are acacias and beech and cedars. Optimistically, perhaps, one is a redwood. Most of them are young, with the exception of a few that stand tall, decades old. The hill, I've learned, was used as a graveyard unofficially for years before it became one formally. Cohen warbles about orgasm and I can see what this place will be in five, ten, a hundred years. A forest of death and rebirth. I've never been one for cemeteries. The cold stone, the hardness of the tombs, the angels, the gargoyles. Monuments to our constructions, not our nature. But here, the air and the fragrance of flowers and leaves. The song finishes and we water the tree. Travis pours two glasses of wine, drinks one and splashes the other over the ground.

Afterward, at Dad's favourite cafe, wine flows liberally, thanks to Travis, and it feels as if something has been released. His ghost, perhaps, no longer trapped in that old cage, whooshing through the walls and floors, asking for his flat white to be extra hot. There's a lot of laughter. Dad laughed a lot. People offer well wishes. Miles's Dad touches my arm and nods, but doesn't stay long. Caelyn's father hugs me harder than he's ever hugged me. When he finally lets me go, he gently slaps me on the cheek. 'You are a fine man, Bren,' he says. 'Your father is proud.' Brenda talks about the decline of the higher education sector until Caelyn rescues me. A man who introduces himself as Rhys tells me I spoke beautifully. I say I'm not sure about that. Rhys puts his hand on my shoulder and says, 'No, mate. That bit about not following in his footsteps, and how he used to get all bent out of shape about it, and how you sat him down one day and said, "Hey, Dad, I love and admire you but I need to be my own person," and he just said "Of course you do, Bren," that was just beautiful, mate. Even if the work you do doesn't make any sense.'

His hand rests on my shoulder a little longer than I'd like. His eyes are glassy. I pat his own shoulder gently, hoping this will break the spell. It doesn't.

'Thanks, Rhys,' I say, 'that's, um, yeah.'

His hand remains on my shoulder. 'Listen,' he says. 'Look after your mother.'

I look over at her. She's surrounded by my aunts and uncles and various well-wishers. She's had a few gins. She looks small, depleted. The enormous burden she's been carrying for years has been lifted, but there's no relief there. 'Yeah,' I say.

Later, Mum, drunk, forces me to dance with her. She says she loves me, Dad loves me and my brother loves me, and she puts her arms around my shoulders and hangs on.

Unusually, I have a face-to-face meeting in a cafe with my colleague Jerez, who I have never met in person. He is beautiful. I've been working with a lot of beautiful people lately. Travis once told me that codified agents were employing human actors to represent them in the workforce. If it's actually true, they've realised that humans really like beautiful humans. Jerez gets us coffee and I catch myself gazing idly at his stunning eyes.

He says that there are problems with the mechanism in the Chatfield Protocol. I can't stop staring at his lips. They are full and voluptuous and mesmerising. I don't know what the Chatfield Protocol is, but I've assigned this work package to him and I don't want to let this beautiful man down. I say, as confidently as I can, 'Okay, what will it take to sort it?'

Jerez takes a second to respond. He says, 'Hmm,' and nods and looks out the window. His face goes blank. Eventually he answers, 'Sorting the mechanism is not a relevant response to the situation, Bren.'

I say, 'Just a bit of slang, Jerez. What will it take to resolve the situation?'

He pauses again. Everything points to this person not being Jerez, but rather someone who is listening as Jerez tells them what to say. After an uncomfortable silence, he says brightly, 'I will require fourteen days of processing resources, thank you!' The person who may or may not be Jerez smiles and looks at me for a long time. I decide to make it more uncomfortable by not saying anything and staring back, just to see how he goes with small talk.

Not well, as it turns out; he soon makes for the exit without a goodbye.

—

I lie on the couch watching a sport I've never seen before. I only watch sports that I can access for free, but there's not many of those left. This sport involves knives, is non-lethal (as far as I can tell) and, according to the confused American commentators, has existed for centuries. No-one is stabbed, but it gets close.

Caelyn arrives home from the library and flops down on the couch. I ask how much she got done and she says that she read a paper about anthropomorphising tennis balls. She hands me an envelope.

'What's this?' I say.

'I dunno. A letter?'

'You opened the mailbox?'

'Thought it was about time. There were dead snails in there.'

The envelope is plain and only partially eaten. The handwriting on it is familiar, but I can't place it.

'Weird, huh?' Caelyn says.

'Weird,' I agree, turning it over.

There is no return address on the back, but there is a sender name: Miles.

Miles was nineteen when he disappeared. We hadn't been friends since primary school. According to his parents, he'd been hanging around with a bad crowd. I never met his new friends; I just saw an occasional photo on social media of dark places and blurred faces. One night Miles went to bed as usual, but the next morning he wasn't there, and he was never seen again. He vanished so completely, it was almost as if had never been there at all. Even his internet presence disappeared. His parents eventually gave up looking and told me if he didn't want to come home he didn't have to. Every now and then they'd give me a call, asking if I'd heard from him. Last time we spoke, I told them that he hadn't been much of a friend and I wouldn't seek him out even if I knew where he was. Mum still talks to them sometimes, but I haven't really thought about him in years.

'Since when do you check the mail?' I say.

Caelyn kicks her legs in frustration and says, 'Open it, open it, open it.'

I do. A slip of paper falls out, along with a blue gum leaf. The note says:

Your brother Miles was here, he loved you, and he has taken root and embraced the bark and the branch and the leaf, and has done so silently and wilfully, for the protection of the earth.

I turn the page in my hands, looking for a hint of something else, anything. But there is nothing.

'Is there an address?' Caelyn asks.

'Can't see one,' I say.

An image forms in my head: Miles at primary school, eight years old or thereabouts, doing an impression of a pelican dance that was popular at the time. 'What happened to him?' I say.

Caelyn shakes her head. 'I can ask some of the communities if you like – see if they know of him.'

'Nah,' I say, 'don't bother.'

—

I don't tell Mum or Miles's parents about the letter because it is the stupidest thing I've ever read.

—

Caelyn puts her book down and says, 'You're seeing a memory.' What I'm actually seeing is her stroking Henry, who has decided for the moment that he likes us. While she's been reading, I've spent what's probably been an hour scanning videos, casts, songs and forums, but when I look up I don't remember any of it.

She says, 'The words that are reaching you are in the past. These words. Right here. By the time you hear them, I'm already somewhere else, thinking about something else. By the time the light of me hits your retinas and travels down your neural pathways to be processed and rendered into an understanding of space by your brain, I'm somewhere else, doing something else.'

'Chances are you're still reading the book,' I say.

She looks at Henry, who closes his eyes and leans into his chin scritches. She says in her catspeak – which is mostly the same way she talks to Penny but with notes of cat – 'It's all happened before, hasn't it, Henno? It's all happened before you're even aware it's happened.'

The cat doesn't open his eyes.

'Don't you see, Bren?' she says with an unsettling smile. 'There is no present. We're only ever touching each other, seeing each other, hearing each other, in the past. I could be a completely different person by the time you hear this.'

I put down my phone and say, 'Probably not much different.'

—

'It doesn't make any sense,' Lila says.

Caelyn laughs and agrees that it doesn't. Aggie says that nothing he's ever done has made sense. Caelyn snorts and Gordo shakes his head, smiling wider. He says it's his shout.

'No, wait,' I say.

Gordo stops.

'Not you – you go get the beers,' I tell him.

Lila says, 'It really doesn't. How could a disembodied alternative intelligence sell a physical product to another disembodied alternative intelligence? And why?'

'Well, that's just it,' I say. 'They aren't disembodied.'

'What,' Aggie says, 'they're robots?'

'No,' I say. 'Well, some probably have the ability to control drones and hardware, but that's not what I'm talking about. I'm talking about them selling products to the human body-proxies of other alternative intelligences.'

Caelyn says, 'They're actors. Bren met one at work.'

'Well, I was pretty sure . . .'

Aggie says, 'Fucking hell.'

Lila chugs her beer and slams the glass on the table. 'Give me an example,' she says.

'Okay,' I say. 'There's a squishy toy that body-proxies can squeeze and it feels nice, but it also releases a calming agent. Because it's a stressful job, and the intelligences understand that body-proxies who are stressed beyond a certain point don't function.'

'So these people are being treated like cats,' Lila says.

'It's just what I've heard,' I say.

'Fucking hell,' Aggie says.

'If this is true,' Lila says, 'why don't we see any of it? Why don't we know about it? It seems like something we would know about.'

'Why would we need to?' I say. 'It's got nothing to do with any of us. It's an entire economy the intelligences are building for themselves. What's so weird is how shit it is. So much crap, like, as smart as they are, they really have no idea what it's like to exist physically in the world. As if a squishy toy is going to fix anything.'

'Fucking hell,' Aggie says.

Caelyn rolls the dice and moves her piece onto a hill overlooking the sea. 'Excellent,' she says in a malicious voice, tapping her fingers together. 'I'm going to build a coastal defence network here and block shipping lanes.'

'That's my whole income stream,' Lila protests.

Caelyn shrugs.

I don't say anything, but like everyone else, I look around the board for other trade routes.

—

'The world flattens you out,' she says.

We've met at a new bar not far from the university. Her supervisor has just given her a stern warning in front of a number of important faculty staff. He told everyone that he thinks her thesis is at best misguided anthropology, at worst fiction.

'I believe in you,' I say. I put my hand on hers.

'You believe *in* me, but you don't *believe* me.' She takes her hand away. 'There's a difference.'

—

Occasionally, someone broadcasts their attempt to become a tree on social media, but they soon get bored or give up when their views go down. From time to time, we hear on the news that a missing person has been found standing in a field in the middle of nowhere. But mostly, no-one's paying attention. There are so many more things to be concerned about.

Caelyn sends me a photo in a message with exclamation marks. It's a tree. A young tree, sure. But just a tree.

I message back, *It's a tree.*

Look closer, she replies.

I magnify the image. There's a vaguely human-like form to one of the limbs, maybe, and the trunk does kind of give the impression of a hip.

She's been looking for months, trying to come up with irrefutable proof that, somewhere, someone has become a tree. There are more tree communities now than there were a few years ago. She's visited several of these little make-believe forests, usually out of the way, usually not far from one of the remaining ancient ones. Every single person there has been convinced that it's going to happen to them, yet there is nothing to suggest this is anything other than a very strange delusion. Her academic colleagues have gone from suspicious to openly mocking. I don't understand why she keeps pursuing this idea so persistently and on the basis of nothing more than a gut feeling. She could present her thesis as an anthropological study of nature-cult behaviour in southern Australia. It would be well received. But something keeps driving her to see things that aren't there, and she's staking an entire career on it. She's right: I don't believe her. The image she's sent me has human-like qualities, sure, but images are so easily doctored, or invented, and trees can take on human features if you look at them hard enough. But clouds can, too. A photo means nothing anymore.

It's still a tree, I say.

She doesn't respond.

—

'You're the only one I have Bren,' she says. 'I'm alone out there. They're threatening to kick me out. I need this. I need *you*.'

I look down at my feet. 'Okay,' I say. 'What can I do to help?'

'Believe me.'

'I've always believed you. I've always supported you. I've always been the guy who is standing here, waiting for . . .'

Her brow furrows. 'Waiting for what?'

I shake my head. 'I don't actually know.'

'It feels a little like you recited that from a movie but got lost halfway,' she says.

I do watch a lot of movies. 'Look, I'll try,' I say. 'But it's hard. I just can't see what you see, and I'm worried for you.'

'Come with me tomorrow. I really think there could be something in this community.'

'You've said that every time. I really think – at some point you're going to have to give up on it. I know it's not what you *want* to hear, Caelyn, but you might *need* to hear it.'

She tenses and clenches her fists, then releases them and breathes out. 'This is the last time. I promise. If nothing comes of it, I'll go crawling on my hands and knees to Gary and tell him that I was trying to construct a fictional meta-commentary on anthropological research or some shite, and that I've decided to revise my approach to something less ground-breaking that won't threaten his own career.'

I grimace. 'You won't word it like that, though,' I say.

'Oh, of course not. Not really. Well, kind of. But no.'

'Okay,' I say. 'One last visit.'

ARBORESCENCE

I make dinner, reassured that after this last, fruitless visit, Caelyn will write a conventional but exceptional thesis, graduate with the University Medal, and have a successful teaching and research career based on perfectly normal subjects like human behaviour.

Westerly, inland, plains of yellow grass, dust, long stretches of asphalt, the occasional abandoned shed, skeletons of trees and distant hills that we never reach. An empty, lifeless land. It's hard to drive through these places and not feel the wreck of it, the ruin, the violence and the removals of its people. There is so much unfinished business.

We drive for hours. 'I haven't seen any birds since we left the coast,' I observe.

—

We stop at a level crossing; the ding ding ding; the horn blasting; the long, snaking cargo train full of whatever it is that people want to move somewhere else. An image I saw in the Queue the other day crosses my mind: it had hair of some kind, probably synthetic; eyes, I think (but it was difficult to tell); and seemed to bleed real blood. It was supposed to represent a character in a briefly popular automatic series that, while still being content-made by its author-generators, the world had long since become indifferent to. The image in the Queue was a knock-off of this character, not even official merchandise. It didn't even look like them. But, somewhere, someone wanted it. Was the train full of these things? These awful, bleeding things?

—

Soon, the night is all around us, and the arms of eucalyptus trees envelop the road. Every now and then we see the glint of eyes reflecting our headlights. Caelyn plays Bongripper, loudly, but I fall asleep anyway.

—

I dream of vines pulling me down, pinning me to the ground, binding me, opening my mouth and stuffing it with leaves and stalks, all the way down my oesophagus to my stomach, my insides bursting with stems and flowers and thorns, bursting from me, bursting out into the world, the rot, the stink of it, my dead flesh exposed and pink and slick, glistening, drying, burning under the sun.

—

She says, 'Bren, we're here.'

I open my eyes to see the sun coming up. We're on a long gravel driveway that ends at a barn, a small, young forest, and a campground of tents, vans and rusting caravans. Another community full of disturbed people pretending to be trees, or caring for people pretending to be trees.

'Time to get to work,' she says.

'No,' I say, rubbing my eyes. 'Coffee.'

She parks the car, gets out to grab her pack and hands me the camera. She's doesn't look at all tired.

'Coffee can wait,' she says. 'And remember, the more photos, the better. I need close-ups of roots, individual leaves, bark. But take some wide-angle shots too. Social stuff. Pictures of the camp and how they've organised themselves. Just in case I need to make this an actual anthropological study.'

'I'll cover you,' I assure her. 'Just in case.'

She gives me a look, but before she can say anything, a person approaches. She has the usual dusty, matted hair, filthy bare feet, and an odour that precedes her by some distance.

Caelyn greets her and says, 'I'm Caelyn, this is Bren. Are you Mika?'

The woman nods shyly.

Caelyn says, 'We talked on the phone. I'm from the university. I'm here to see Oscar.'

Mika purses her lips and looks back at the camp, where a few dozen people watch us. The communities are always suspicious. They usually hide themselves away. Several have been dispersed: by police, by loggers, by men with guns and trucks, by irritated graziers who've decided their sheep suddenly need the space. Caelyn's worked hard to gain their trust.

'Oh,' Mika says. 'Oh. I probably wasn't clear on the phone.'

And here it is, finally. Caelyn's shoulders droop. She's been tilting at windmills for a while now. It's been month after month of disappointment. This is her last chance. And if I'm honest, my heart beats a little faster, knowing it's about to come. I'm not proud of it, but I want this fantasy to be over. I don't want her to be sad, I don't want her career to founder before it's even begun, but she has stubbornly pursued a delusion. There's no other outcome here. This is clearly a social phenomenon, as her supervisor says. She needs to focus on the realities of it: that something is driving people to withdraw from human society. A viral mental illness, perhaps, or something like it, but nothing more. Relief pours through me.

'He's left, has he?' Caelyn says.

'No, he's in town,' Mika says.

Caelyn frowns. 'Oh. I thought he was . . . you know. Has he gone shopping?'

Mika laughs loudly, catches herself and puts her hand over her mouth. 'No, no,' she says. 'He just wanted to dig in near the river. He always said the reason others were failing was that they were trying to dig in to the wrong spots. Like this barren field.' She smiles. 'So he dug in next to the river.'

'*Dug in,*' Caelyn repeats. 'What does the town think?'

Mika shrugs. 'We're all here,' she says. She looks over her shoulder. There's not much activity in the camp; a few people sit on chairs, drinking, eating or reading. 'Well, most of us. But we're going to join him,' she says. 'We're thinking about moving the camp.'

'Mind if I take a few photos?' I say.

'Sure,' Mika says. 'We don't have anything to hide.'

I glance at Caelyn. The air around her now has become electric. Her shoulders lift and colour returns to her cheeks. She thinks a door is about to open. She speaks hesitantly. 'Did it take?' she asks.

'Did what take?' Mika says.

'Did he, you know, change?'

Mika smiles patiently. 'Of course,' she says. 'He was a landscape gardener. Did permaculture stuff. He knew what he was doing. Taught us a few things too.'

Carefully, conscious that her future hangs in the balance, aware of how quickly doors can be closed, how a word or a poorly stated intention might lock them forever, Caelyn asks, 'Can you take us to him?'

—

'What happened?' Caelyn says. She's talking to Mika, recording and taking notes while I drive.

'What do you mean?' says Mika.

'What made you all decide to leave and . . . you know.'

Mika responds kindly, as if she's speaking to a child. 'What made us want to surrender?'

Caelyn almost jumps at the word. 'Is that what you call it? Surrendering?'

'Sure,' Mika says. 'It's like a surrender where everyone wins, you know? Like a war where both sides just stop fighting and become friends again.'

'That's so interesting,' Caelyn says.

'But,' I say, aware that I'm not supposed to speak in these situations but finding it difficult to contain myself, 'trees and humans aren't at war.'

They both laugh.

'Tell that to the bones of the trees in your house,' Mika says.

The town is a hamlet, really, with no-one in sight. It would have once served the farming community, but now there are vacant houses, shops, sheds full of rusting machinery and overgrown grass.

'How long's it been like this?' I ask, snapping some photos. Mika says, 'I don't know. A year, maybe?'

The river is lined by many trees: mostly oaks, elms and maple closer to the town, giving way to river gums, she-oaks, and wattle on the outskirts. Many of them have clearly been here for centuries. Mika takes us to an overgrown park on the riverbank. I say that it could use a mow. Mika scowls and says sharply, 'We don't believe in mowers.'

'You said before that all the town left? You're all at the camp?' Caelyn says.

'Yep,' Mika says. 'Well, there were a couple who didn't join us. They own the petrol station. Said it wasn't right to deprive travellers of their right to travel. It was their duty to keep the arteries of human civilisation flowing. Anyway, here's Oscar.'

What had I been expecting? Nothing. Well, no, maybe not nothing. I was expecting her to say that any one of these trees was, in fact, a human. That she would choose one at random, point to it, say that's him, and it would just be a tree and we'd take some notes and some photos and go home. Caelyn would be disappointed, but she would finally see sense, and she'd finish writing her PhD about strange human behaviours and get a regular academic job and it'd all be very normal.

But that's not what happens.

Mika approaches a tree that is separate from others on the riverbank. It's an oak that's perhaps a few decades old. She kneels next to it and puts her hand on the bark. 'Hi, Oscar,' she says. She runs her hand over the trunk as if looking for something. At the base there's a small plaque that reads: *Oscar Parrington, who loves the earth.* And I don't know why or how I know, but I know. This is not just a tree. The ground at its feet hasn't been underneath an oak tree for that long. It's disturbed, light, with no debris, or grass or a bed of leaves; it hasn't settled into and around the tree's roots. My mind finds it hard to reconcile, as if I'm not really seeing what I'm seeing.

Caelyn is watching intently. She says, 'May I approach?'

Mika nods. 'Of course, but be gentle. He's still young.'

'Decent trunk girth,' Caelyn says. 'Decades old.'

Mika says, 'That's the way it works.'

'Yes,' Caelyn says. 'That seems to be the case elsewhere too. The tree forms as if it is as old as the person. How old was he?'

'Thirty-three.' Mika adds, 'Look out for the roots there. I don't think he likes people standing on the roots.'

Caelyn takes a step back. 'Have you talked to him? I mean, did he tell you he doesn't like people standing on his roots?'

'We chat,' Mika says, 'but it's only one way. It's just good manners.'

Caelyn smiles and says, 'Sure, sure.'

I look up at the boughs, thick arms reaching for the sky. The bark, the skin. There's no obvious humanity here. No weirdly stretched skin, evidence of hair or muscle or bone. This isn't something from a horror movie, even though it's making me feel like I'm in one. There's no hidden face in the trunk, no eyes peering out from a branch. And yet it's not quite a tree either. There's something about its leaves, its bark. A different pallor, or texture. I pick up an acorn and inspect it. It's pale green, and the seed gives a little when I squeeze it. A little too much. It's not fleshy, but it doesn't quite feel like an acorn either. As if it were created too quickly to accumulate its usual density. A shiver passes through my body. There is something so grotesque, so unnatural happening here. I swiftly return the acorn the ground and wipe my hands on my pants.

'So,' I say, 'did he change overnight? Was he standing here, a human person, and the next day you saw him he was this?'

Mika gives me a strange look. 'Oh no,' she says. 'It took longer than that. A few weeks. A few weeks of standing as still as he could, rejecting everything his muscle-body was saying. No moving, no eating, as little breathing as possible. He was drawing a breath only once every five minutes in the last few days.'

'It's like meditation,' Caelyn says.

Mika shakes her head vigorously. 'No, it's more. It requires a complete abandonment of the human. But our body betrays us, tries to bring us back. Always twitching, always needing, always wanting to move, to shape. So we built little supports for him. Gave him water. Nurtured him. Just until he dug in. And then the roots started to form from his feet. It only took a few days after that.' She looks at the tree and caresses the bark. 'It was hard to watch, that last part. It hurt. You could tell. The noises he was making. Not animal at all. Something else. Something groaning and resisting and aching. And then it stopped.'

Caelyn leans down and brushes the roots.

'Do you miss him?' I ask, because I'm pretty sure this is a man who has become a tree and that's all I can think of to say.

'He hasn't gone anywhere.'

A few metres above, embedded in the trunk, I see what looks to be the brim of a baseball cap. The rest of the hat appears to have been swallowed by the bark.

'Is that a hat?' I say.

Caelyn looks to where I'm pointing. She studies the brim. 'Boston Red Sox,' she says.

'I wanted him to be sun smart,' Mika says. 'Just in case. He always said I never had enough faith. Said I'd never dig in and thrive unless I had faith. He put it on anyway. The bark lifted it off his head and swallowed it, the way it swallowed him.'

'Swallowed,' I say, imagining bark moving like water over this man with the Boston Red Sox hat. 'So he, um, liked baseball?'

'Was he scared?' Caelyn ask. 'When it happened?'

'I don't think so. He wasn't able to move or talk, but he didn't seem scared. When the first root appeared between his toes, I could swear I saw his face lighten. Like the sun was shining on it for the first time. His muscles relaxed. It was like he was released of something.'

'Wait,' I say. 'Is he still in there? Did his body dissolve or whatever, or is it just – what did you call it? Swallowed? Like, if someone cut it down, would there be bones and –'

Caelyn puts her hand over my mouth and says, 'Shut the fuck up, Bren.'

Mika smiles patiently again and looks up at the branches that tower above us. She says, 'This is Oscar.'

—

We take Mika back to the camp. While I pack up to go home, Caelyn announces she's going to stay.

'I have to, Bren,' Caelyn says. 'You know I have to. Finally I'll be able to go to that monthly meeting with Gary and say, *Hey, dude, fuck you. Here's what I've been trying to show you, and if you'd just listened you could have been in on it too, you could have exploited me like you exploit all your promising candidates, taking their ideas and presenting them as your own, but instead I'll be famous with this thesis and present it at conferences everywhere and you'll be left behind.*' She takes a breath.

'Whoa,' I say. 'You make it sound like academia is some kind of lottery you've just won.'

She smirks. 'It isn't? But yeah, I know. I'm just excited.'

'How long do you think?'

'Dunno. A few weeks.' She lowers her voice to a whisper. 'I'm going to need to get some samples. You know. For testing. I'm not going to convince anyone with photos.'

'What do you mean, samples?' I whisper back.

'I'll just go down there one night discreetly and grab some bark and leaves. Harmless.'

Mika talks quietly to a group sitting at trestle tables. They look over at us and nod. 'Be careful,' I say.

'If they start trying to plant me in the ground, all I have to do to stop it is wiggle a pinkie toe, right?'

'Yeah,' I say. 'Yeah, okay.'

The camp has about a hundred people. There's no open fire here, but there are solar panels on every surface. Someone cooks on what looks to be an electric stove. Mika comes over and says to Caelyn, 'They're happy for you to stay in one of the spare tents. And for you to talk, record, write, whatever. We don't see the need to keep quiet about this. Not after Oscar. The world needs to know that there's a better way to be part of the earth.'

I look at Caelyn, who looks back at me. She's full of sparks. The dark rings around her eyes betray her lack of sleep, but otherwise she looks more energised than I've seen her for some time. The moment that passes between us is heavy. It's a sudden pull away, a tiny crack, a fault line. Something has shifted in our understanding of the world. I can smell the air in a way I haven't smelled it before. Earthy, fragrant, foreign. Like a scent that's always been there but that I've only just noticed. She smells it too. It excites her, this change. This re-reckoning with reality. She will stay here and rebuild her understanding. I will drive home. I will go back to work. And I will try to hold on to what I can, for as long as I can.

I say, 'Show them what you can do.' I draw her close and she hugs me so tightly I'm almost winded.

—

I'm exhausted, so on the way home I stop for the night at a country motel. In the evening light, I wander the quiet main street. I find a Chinese restaurant open, a relic of a time in which the only restaurants in most towns were Chinese or Italian. I order lemon chicken and fried rice. I wander back to the motel, doing my best to ignore the stares and mutterings of the damp, flushed men drinking outside the pub. In my room, I play video games on my phone while the television plays an old episode of *Investigatore Polizia*. It's the one where Inspector Elena Polizia discovers her police chief father was actually a famous serial killer known as The Wrangler. Mostly, though, it's about her going on bad dates, which is strange, because I don't know if I would want to go on dates if I just found out my father was a mass murderer who had escaped police custody and was hunting me down for some reason. It's a mess of a show all around, as if seven different plots had been written and abandoned halfway through, but perhaps that's actually close to real life. Perhaps I have judged *Investigatore Polizia* unfairly this whole time. Perhaps this is a clever commentary on the artificiality of traditional dramatic structures, how they are normally constructed to appeal to audiences rather than accurately reflect human existence. Of course, this would mean that the writers of this low-budget Italian cop drama had full awareness that they were repudiating millennia of dramatic theory, which, given Investigatore Polizia tells a junior colleague that books are for people with too much time on their hands, they probably weren't.

This is incredible, she texts me one night. *More of them are trying. I might get to see it happen.*

—

I join Travis on his work trip. He's spruiking a cool climate shiraz and pinot noir from a coastal winery not far out of the city. As the day goes on and he talks to more wine merchants, I realise that I'm the designated driver. He says it's nice not having to spit it out for once. After the last meeting, he tells me to stop in a car park by the beach, says he misses Dad, and cries. He demands I take him to Dad's tree.

We drive over to the cemetery, and Travis takes two bottles of his most expensive cabernet sauvignon and pours them over the tree.

'I'm not sure that's good for it, Trav,' I say.

'Wine is good for everyone,' he says. 'It's like water but better.'

—

When I'm old, I wonder if I'll remember how it felt to move so easily through the world.

'We're monkeys,' she says to me on the phone one night. Caelyn has been at the camp a few days now and occasionally visiting the abandoned pub for a drink. There's still mobile reception in town, even though no-one needs it. 'Monkeys,' she slurs, 'and we, my darling, my love, my sweetle-blossom, belong in the trees.'

'I thought we were supposed to *be* trees,' I say. 'According to these people, at least.'

'No!' she exclaims. 'No no no. Not everyone is a tree. Not everyone has the ability or the patience. Even if they want to, they can't. Listen, Bren. In the last few days, three more people have arboresced.'

'Arboresced?' I say.

'That's what I'm calling it. Well, they call it that. But I'm going to use it. It's nice, don't you think? But the point is, not everyone is a tree. Some are just monkeys. But there needs to be more trees and fewer monkeys. Doesn't it make sense? All these monkeys all over the world throwing their shit around, and all these poor trees just like going, what the fuck, man?' I hear a bottle slam onto a wooden table. 'Aw, shit. Just a sec, I got to –' I hear some things shuffling around. 'Yeah, like all these trees going, what the fuck? Why you gotta cut us down and burn us and throw all your shit around? And Christmas, what the fuck is that? Didn't you ever read Hans Christian Andersen? The cognitive dissonance of these fucking monkeys. Running around, ruining everything. Just wish they'd stop. You know?'

'You're anti-monkey now?'

'Naw,' she says, 'no way. I love monkeys. Their little faces.'

—

Three weeks later she texts me to say that she has her samples, her videos and her interviews. *Just a little longer*, she says.

—

Bowden tells me on a chat window to monitor my throughput. I say that my throughput is thoroughly monitored. They don't respond. Not for the first time I wonder if messages from him are automated. The next item in the Queue is a request for an interview with the moderately well-known singer Clarice Quail. The credibility and influence score of the applicant is low, but not low enough to reject it outright. The current impact score of Quail indicates potential for limited growth, and the report recommends exposure to any kind of media, regardless of CI score. I pass the request on to Gundar, who, as always, thanks me more than he needs to.

—

The next work package in the Queue is a design for an imaginary city called 'Hopetopia' that someone wants printed in 1:1 scale. The city has been designed beautifully. It's full of leafy streets, bustling pedestrian districts, parks, glassy domes, rooftop bars, tropical plants and waterfalls. I'm not sure if anyone is capable of printing a city to 1:1 scale, or where it will be placed if it is printed. The logistics are poorly thought through. It's hard to say where these requests come from. Perhaps a bored trillionaire's kid who fails to understand – or doesn't care – that utopian cities require dystopian conditions elsewhere. Still, the Queue demands it be attended to. I assign it to Pierre, who usually classifies work packages he receives as not feasible and is shameless about it. He hasn't processed a package completely for several months. Hopetopia won't be built any time soon.

—

The next work package in the Queue is asking for the definition of a cloud. I don't understand why these sorts of packages come through when they often take just a simple online search. It's probably another bored rich person who has run out of people to boss around. I assign it to Iona, who completes the request in thirty seconds and says, *Have you ever heard of formesteen?*

—

Sitting in the cafe before work, I suddenly remember that people are becoming trees. It's not like I don't already know this, not after seeing Oscar and the disturbing videos Caelyn's been sending – the way the body gets absorbed by bark is not something I need to see again – but my mind has buried it. I guess it's cognitive dissonance, like she said. I've been going to work, going to the football with my brother, watching television shows, as if nothing has changed. And I know that everything has changed, but something in my body, my soul, my brain, refuses to accept it. I look at the painting of the tree on the wall over the road from the cafe. Is the artist a tree now? What makes someone want to become a tree? Wait – people are becoming trees? It's a surprise every time I think about it.

—

The next work package in the Queue is for a bold work of experimental fiction from an exciting new writer who will go on to win many awards and become the darling of the literary scene. It has to feature a protagonist called Misty, who is really beautiful, and sleeps with whoever she wants, and they all love her but she doesn't need them. There should be swords involved, but not blood. A mountain must feature in at least five scenes. The protagonist called Misty has an enemy called Susan, who has always given her the shits. It will be fast-paced but lyrical and poetic. The reader should always be excited, but also reflect on their life a lot, mostly because of how Misty is really prescient. It will have a noir vibe, but with a beige 1970s style. There should be an edge, but not too sharp, and it should be suitable for a beach read. It should be the sort of book to sell at least 50,000 copies. It must not be more than three hundred pages but should have many layers and themes. Themes should include romance, adventure, crime, beaches and swords. Misty will end up saving the world in a particular typeface. It should change the way we think. It should reconfigure what fiction is capable of doing. It shouldn't be too hard to read. The author's name should also be Misty, and they should be award-winning, and they will end up dying in an opium den because they can't contain their own genius.

I give this one to Iona, who again mentions formesteen. She returns the request in thirty seconds.

—

A text from Caelyn: *I suspect there's a whole social contract that's going to form around the age of the person when they "dig in", as they put it. If this becomes something that takes hold in the wider community, the implications are fascinating.*

I've been getting a lot of these texts. *Wait*, I message back, *why would it take hold in the wider community?*

She replies, *Why wouldn't it?*

—

The next work package in the Queue is a promotional video for a piece of silicone that looks like a penis but is not a sex toy because written on its base are the words: *Not for sex use*. Raymond does well with these ones, so over it goes. His video suggests that it is a cooking utensil for extracting the annoying fibres from ginger. I don't know if he's right, but he posts it anyway and the request doesn't come back.

—

Caelyn appears one day in the living room, beaming, smelling terrible. She puts down her backpack and says, 'Done!'

She opens her arms for a hug, but I shake my head and say, 'It's been so long. I've – well, I've moved on.' I call out to the kitchen, 'Ella! You should meet my old girlfriend. You know, the one who disappeared for six weeks.'

Caelyn's arms fall and she shoots a glance at the kitchen. Henry walks out lazily and yells something. Caelyn squeals and picks him up. 'Okay, Henry,' she says, cradling the protesting cat in her arms, 'your roommate here is a nasty fucker. But it's good to see you, boy. It's so good to see you.' Henry doesn't buy it and wriggles out of her grip.

—

Caelyn talks and talks and shows me grotesque videos of arborescence. She's fascinating and funny and I can't take my eyes off her. We open a bottle of wine and she tells me about the community, how an eighty-year-old man became a thick, gnarled river gum, how it grew like something out of 'Jack and the Beanstalk', like it was CGI. The pain of it, the awful sound, the ripping of bark and flesh and vocal cords. But then, the transcendence. The peace.

After a few hours of talking and showing me videos, she lies back on the floor next to her still-packed backpack. 'One night I asked a few of them why they were doing it,' she says. 'A guy told me, "It's the right thing to do." The others all agreed. He said they couldn't explain it any other way.'

—

I order two batches of formesteen. I track it for weeks. I see it bob up and down on the ship. When it finally arrives, Caelyn asks what it is. I say it's a supplement, I guess. She asks what it's supplementing, and I say that I don't know. I put it away and we don't mention it again.

—

We watch a show while Henry hunts a fly. I'm starting to think it's the same story, over and over. We've been copying the ancient Greeks for thousands of years, while ignoring the ancient storytellers of our own land. Introduction, inciting incident, rising action, here we go, here's the music that indicates the fall, here's the music that indicates the next fall, wait, a rise, but it's not enough, a fall again, but wait, the next rise, the real rise, and we know, from the start, from the beginning of the whole hundred-hour exercise, how it will end, more or less. Over and over, the same story repeated. As if it's the only way we want to understand the world, as if we can't submit to its chaos. As if, by giving existence a false sense of order, we have bent it to our will. And when it's over, what have we done but rendered the world imperfectly, reductively; simplified it beyond truth, made it linear, made it a straight line from dots on a page, made connections where there are none, escaped to something with rules that make sense, escaped from this planet careening through space, escaped this baffling, insensible entropy that assails us, these disconnections, these echoes of time and memory and sensation; a fly on the wall with its compound eyes seeing things refracted and reflected, a different world – what did that person call it? *umwelt* – Henry staring at it crawling up the wall, another world again, another chaotic insensible place, and he pounces and catches it underneath his paw. A world extinguished by another. A compound eye not enough to spy the threat. The same story, over and over.

'I don't know if you've displayed a full grasp of the history of storytelling there,' Caelyn says. 'It's just a show about space chefs.'

—

Rita says I undercut everything serious I say with humour and so lose the impact of the serious thing I say. I tell her she needs to get the package done by close of business.

—

'They still don't fucking believe me,' Caelyn spits.

'Yes,' I say, 'but I really need to finish my laps.'

I push off the pool wall. As usual I end up in a lane that isn't my own. I'm not a great swimmer. When I get out of the water, she accosts me again. She dressed in the time it took me to swim two laps.

'Gary keeps saying the videos don't prove anything. Reckons you can easily fake it. That if my research held up, he would submit a paper on pigs flying over Lord's Cricket Ground. And the lab says the DNA samples were contaminated because they contain a mix of plant and animal matter. Of course they fucking do! That's the point!'

I get my towel and dry myself off. 'So make it about that,' I say. 'The inability of the traditional scientific method and academia to cope with modern situations.'

She repeats, 'They still don't fucking believe me.'

ARBORESCENCE

—

There's always the seed of an arc, sometimes more than one, planted at the start of the story. I've seen so many of these stories I recognise it when I see it. That shot of the gun, that's important. Oh, she put that in her pocket. That'll be important. And when it comes back later, we act surprised. Oh, the gun, we remark. She remembered the gun. Phew. Or: Oh no! She forgot the gun! Now *he's* got the gun! But we start applying these shapes to our own lives, get disappointed when the romance falters, when the dreams shatter, when the paper in the back pocket turns out to be just a blank piece of paper and not the answer to the riddle of the ancient zombie vampire dragon tomb. We live normal, vibrant lives, but we wish there were arcs, we wish we were something else. We wish we were heroes. But there are no arcs. There are no story beats. We hurtle through space, alive. Why isn't it enough?

—

Caelyn comes home from university, flops on the couch and puts a blanket over her head. This has been happening a lot. I make some dinner and she eats it underneath the blanket. She says between bites that they're making her write a normal thesis for normal people and you saw that, Bren, it happened, and I say that I saw the videos, and it did, and I say maybe they aren't ready, and she says, 'Of course they're not ready, fucking ivory tower pieces of shit.'

'So are you going to be able to write a normal thesis for normal people in the next six months?'

'I've got a backup ready to go.'

'You've got a backup. A whole thesis as a backup. You wrote two theses.'

'I'm just not happy about having to submit it. I can still keep trying to further the research in this area. But to get my PhD, I'm going to have to play their game.' She comes out from beneath the blanket, pasta sauce all over her face. 'Oh,' she says, 'Mika also got in touch with me today, and . . . I think I might know where Miles is.'

'What?'

'She told me about an older community in the north. She said they were more spiritual in their thinking. Sent out letters to people they cared for to let them know when they were digging in.'

'So?'

'What do you mean, so? I'm going up there next week.'

'You have a thesis to write.'

'I told you, it's nearly done. I'm focusing on the postdoc now. When people realise this is real. Will you come along? Road trip?'

'I don't need to see Miles,' I say. 'Whatever he is.'

But I go anyway.

This time, we visit a camp that has formed near an old plantation of Californian redwood. These trees don't grow here normally, but a few centuries ago, someone decided that they should. They are young, as redwood go. A hundred years old, maybe two hundred. But together, even in the carefully planted rows, they evoke the sense of a cathedral. It's not like encountering them in the forests of North America – there's no real undergrowth, and there's something eerie and too ordered about it. I've always wondered what trees that aren't native to a region think, or feel, or sense, when they are planted in foreign soil. Are they confused? Or do they just get on with it?

—

The small camp is situated at the edge of the plantation, near a few trees of all kinds and ages that seem less established. There's no evidence of fire or cooking, no sign of heat. They scowl as we approach. The usual story. Caelyn says she's a friend of Mika, from one of the communities in the west. That puts them at ease and they invite us to sit. I study the redwoods that tower over the camp, but I don't see anything I'm looking for.

Caelyn talks about the other community. She tells them about Oscar, and how several others have joined him. It's progressing well, she says. This pleases them. After offering them some coffee from our thermos, which they accept greedily, she asks: 'Did you know Miles Zan?' A middle-aged woman smiles wistfully and says, 'Yes, he was one of the first.' She looks over my shoulder. I follow her gaze to a young redwood.

—

As kids, Miles and I liked comic books. But we loved *Voidstar*. We'd walk down to the local comic book store every week to see if a new issue had come out. If it had, we'd take it back to my place and pore over it together. It consumed us.

Voidstar was a walking universe who took different forms every issue. They might be a person, an idea, a forest, a lake, a star. They were genderless, ageless, and indifferent to both the universe they were in and the universe inside them. The comic books continued to be published for decades, written by one man, Irving Shrike, a Californian recluse who gave only three interviews in his lifetime. The series spawned multiple screen adaptations, most of which weren't very good. Voidstar went everywhere: to earth, sometimes, but so many more places. There were underwater cities on distant moons; ruined planet-sized architectures being consumed by three suns; discworlds with unusual gravity; planets in waterfalls; spires of cellular networks; plant worlds; bridges; arteries; blood; air. A dizzying array of worlds, microscopic or so large they defied imagination, and

Voidstar would be there, usually indifferent to it all. Conflict between the universe inside Voidstar and the universe they passed through was frequent and monumental, and yet Voidstar was mostly oblivious to it. They were many, they rarely spoke, and they acted in ways that rarely made sense. They were completely unaware of the ripples they made. They were the gentlest chaos.

Whoa, we'd say. A world in a spire reaching into some distant, nebulous heaven. A single tiny spider terrorising a city. A coin-sized cosmic rock weighing more than the planet it was hurtling toward and bound to destroy. My brain would be dazzled with possibility. Miles would sometimes take a break and lie on his back and say that Voidstar was cool, and I knew what he meant, because Voidstar *was* cool – aloof but wise when they eventually communicated. But I didn't care so much about Voidstar. It was more the places they travelled through, destroyed or united. I would talk endlessly about spinning buildings or gravity wells or civilisations hidden under beds; Miles would focus on Voidstar and the form they had taken and say he wished he could do that. 'Any shape, any time, just disappear,' he said. 'Just be, like, here but not here, like no-one would bother you, you know?' I said, 'Yeah, for sure, but how cool is this?'

—

'Name's Helena,' the woman says, as she takes us to an impressive but young redwood. 'I wasn't here at the time, but I heard Miles was a lovely fella.' There's a plaque at the base of the tree. It reads: *Miles Zan, who believes in the earth.* The bark is thick and heavy. It hasn't got the uncanny, spongy feeling Oscar's did. This hasn't happened recently. Or it's a lie.

I can sense Caelyn looking at me. 'Why would you make something like this up?' I say.

Helena puts her hand on the trunk. 'I think,' she says, 'you answered your own question.'

'I don't know what you're trying to pull here, but it's bullshit.' Heat rises in me and I punch the tree, a little harder than I should. 'Ow,' I say.

Caelyn reaches for me but I stomp off, because I can feel him there; I know he is there.

—

Voidstar on a floating structure, like a pier, but not connected to any land, in the middle of a raging sea that threatens to sink it.

—

The sun pours over my head as I lie in the grass. I hear footsteps approach. Someone lies next to me. I can smell her: her neck, her hair, that slight breeze of skin and sky and sour that I crave, that I nuzzle up to on cold nights when all I can feel is my bones freezing, seizing up, becoming glaciers. 'I loved him,' I say.

'I know,' she says.

'Maybe I was a shit friend. Or I was just there. Maybe he got sick of me. Maybe it was all one way. Maybe I was too much.'

Her body shifts a little closer, not enough to touch but enough to know. 'Bren,' she says, 'you were kids. People do things they regret. He thought enough of you to send you a letter about, well, this. It doesn't sound one way.'

We lie there for a little longer.

'You know this is all complete bullshit,' I say. 'They killed him or he killed himself or whatever, and they buried him and put a plaque next to this tree. We should call the police.'

Caelyn says calmly, 'I don't think so.'

Moments pass. I can feel the shadow of a cloud pass over my head.

'Thing is,' I say, 'I can feel him there. It's probably wishful thinking, or maybe the opposite of wishful thinking. How am I supposed to tell his family about this?'

The sunlight fades completely. I open my eyes to a blue twilight.

Caelyn is sitting up, cross-legged, watching me. 'Come on,' she says, offering her hand. 'They're cooking us dinner.'

—

Voidstar was a traveller without purpose, without direction. The comics surprised us, over and over. You'd expect to see a character fall and instead they would rise. Characters would disappear from the narrative suddenly only to reappear in a crowd four years later but remain unrecognisable to anyone but the reader. There was no throughline, no plot. There Voidstar was, at the foot of the mesa, fighting alongside the Olfactory Reservists. There they were, at the Diamond Oasis, watching as two traders negotiated a deal over their respective rock dust.

Worlds upon worlds, people upon people, arriving and just as quickly leaving. It was deeply frustrating for many readers to see the clear and potentially dramatically satisfying narrative paths not taken, replaced by these aimless, pointless meanderings. But we were always enthralled. We obsessed over each new issue, and wondered where they would go next, what universes they would crack open.

—

The camp is similar to the other communities I've been to, but a little more established. The structures are weather-beaten and well lived in. The tyres on the caravans are flat and there's a lot of rust. Strings of lights hang from branches. Someone plays the guitar softly, hums, stops, then plays it again. In the distance, not too far from the camp, a dozen or so people stand in silence. 'More hopefuls,' I say to Caelyn, and she nods.

We're taken to a communal table in a big tent and given food and drink that isn't terrible. The conversation, as is often the case, centres around plants. I clumsily inject a reference to politics – the US president is once again a concern – but no-one laughs. I mention that I work with people who are probably robots and they all smile and shake their heads and go back to talking about fertiliser. I say to the woman next to me that I can't believe they've incorporated bats into football now, and she says that's animal cruelty. I begin to explain that I'm talking about cricket bats, but she isn't interested. I'm not sure I have the right conversational tools to speak to these people. Caelyn takes notes and records them talking and they don't mind. Part of me is thrilled that somewhere in her research archive will be a recording of me and another person confusing the word 'bat'.

They let us stay the night. We settle into one of the caravans left behind by someone.

'Where'd they go?' Caelyn asks.

'Over there,' the grizzled old man says, looking at a redwood not far from the camp. 'Enjoy your rest,' they say.

Caelyn whispers, 'Why do you think these people are deciding to become redwoods?'

'How do you know they get a choice?' I say. 'Maybe our tree genetics are a latent part of our DNA just waiting to be triggered. Maybe you're a spruce and I'm a Norfolk pine.'

'I don't think that's how it works.'

'Well, you're the scientist, you tell me.'

'I'm not a scientist,' she says.

'Then what are you?' I say.

She looks at me for a long time before saying, 'You know, I'm not really sure.'

—

It's dark and everyone is asleep.

I leave the caravan and sit with my back against the trunk.

'Remember when Voidstar met this kid who kept commenting on everything he saw? Like, he'd read out the signs they were passing, or mention how the road is really windy or something? And this whole issue was just Voidstar and this kid walking somewhere, and this kid talking and Voidstar saying nothing, until the very end when the kid asks why they don't say anything.

And Voidstar looks at him, and it's one of those close-ups where you can kind of see the whole universe behind their eyes, and says that words are an imperfect form of communication. That it should be enough just to move through time and space with another being for a while. And the kid disagrees; completely misses the point. I think they wind up in a casino; I don't remember. I guess what I'm saying is that it doesn't matter if you're there.'

The night is cool but not cold, the camp is quiet, and the stars out here give just enough light to see by. The bed of redwood needles I'm sitting on is surprisingly comfortable. I try not to think of spiders.

'What happened to you in high school? You made me feel like a piece of shit. Absolute rock bottom. I wasn't sure I was going to get out of it. You were a monster. And then you just faded away. And honestly, I don't know why I'm here looking for you. You're the one who left. You're the one who should be explaining yourself. Your parents were probably shitheads or something, like you used to say. But still. They deserved to know. Didn't they? Maybe they didn't. Maybe it was that bad. You could have said something, though. Talked to me.'

I pick up a cone and throw it at another tree. Another former person, I suppose. It hits, and I get the feeling that the Miles-tree approves.

'But maybe you did, and I wasn't listening.'

Something rustles in the leaves above me. A bird, perhaps, or a possum.

'You always spoke so quietly.'

I breathe in the cool night air, filled with the smell of conifers.

'Good choice of tree,' I say. 'Redwood. I'd have thought you'd have gone for a native. Guess I didn't know you that well.'

My back, resting against his rough bark, is getting uncomfortable.

'Listen, I'm done now, okay? No more. You don't get any more space in my head. This was your choice. I'm done with it.'

I jump up, pat the trunk and walk back to the sad little caravan.

Caelyn murmurs, 'You okay?' as I crawl into bed.

'Yeah,' I say. 'Just needed to get a few things off my chest. I don't know if it's really him, though.'

She puts her arms around my waist, spooning me from behind. She kisses the back of my neck and whispers in my ear, 'I'm going to find out.'

—

A woman named Aksha hands me a thick journal, battered and stuffed with what seems to be leaves, stems, bookmarks, postcards, photos and twine. She says, 'He wanted you to have this.'

'He mentioned me specifically?' I say.

'Well, no. Just that if someone came to give it to them.' She looks at her feet. 'He was, um, he's good. He's happier this way.'

I look over at the tree masquerading as my one-time friend.

'I'll look after him,' she says. 'We'll look after him.'

'You aren't going to follow?'

'I'm not ready yet,' she says. 'It hurts. It hurts a lot. But by the time it really begins hurting, you can't talk or move.'

'Then how do you know it hurts?'

'You can tell,' she says. 'It's in their face.'

'Christ,' I say.

'But then it stops and they are so relieved. Maybe more relieved than they've ever been. I'll get there soon. I just have to learn to still myself.'

'This feels like death,' I say. 'Like you're all choosing to die.'

She looks at me with great concern and puts her hand on mine. 'Oh sweetheart, no,' she says. 'This is a chance for another life.'

'Are there drugs involved?'

She laughs, a little maniacally, exactly the way someone would if they had been taking lots of drugs. 'We stay off substances beforehand. We don't know what they might do. Listen, I'll take care of him.' She puts her hand on my shoulder.

'But how, if you're another tree?'

She smiles and says, 'Then I'll be able to take care of him even more.'

—

'These people are on so many drugs,' I say, as we drive away.

'Maybe,' Caelyn says cryptically. 'But probably not the ones we think.'

I shake my head and say, 'Do you ever get tired of confusing me?'

A bright summer morning. That blue sky, the yellow-green light, almost luminescent, of the robinia trees that line our street. Another successful invader. There's a lilt to the air, a syrup; it feels intoxicating. I'm walking to my temporary office, which I've now leased for several years. There's talk of a restructure in the Queue. There have been a few already. I've been coordinating several difficult but incredibly attractive employees for some time. I think it might be something I'm expected to fail in. The Queue has been getting more and more nonsensical.

Outside Neko's cafe I spy the artist who painted the mural of the tree all those years ago. He's standing with his arms at his side, eyes closed. I ask Neko how long he's been there and he says a week.

'A full week?' I say.

And he says, 'I've watched the camera. He never fucking leaves. Occasionally someone pours water over him or hoses him down. He should be dead.' He hands me my cup.

'Fuck,' I say.

'Yeah,' he says.

I sip the coffee and we watch him together without speaking. 'He doesn't even move,' I say.

'Yeah,' he says.

'It's spreading,' I say.

'Yeah,' he says. 'I mean, what?'

The artist looks peaceful.

My phone buzzes. I reach down without taking my eyes off the standing man.

A message from Caelyn: *I didn't want to tell you anything before, but at your Dad's wake, I grabbed a glass Miles's dad had been drinking from. I got it tested and I've been waiting six months for the results. They just came through. Miles's DNA is almost certainly in that tree. I want to say I'm sorry, but I'm not sure that's the right response. Talk at home xxxx*

I look up at the artist, frozen, stilled, waiting. 'It's spreading,' I repeat.

—

'Listen, Mum,' I say. 'It's about Miles. Caelyn took some samples and found a DNA match with his dad. There's no doubt he either *is* this tree or is *in* this tree.'

She looks as if she's been made to drink lemon juice. 'What would make you say something like that, Bren? Ugh. I need to get ready for church.'

She's never been to church. Not once in all the years I've known her. But now that Dad's gone, something's shifted. She felt uncomfortable about him having a secular funeral, but only said so months after the fact and blamed Travis and me for Dad's godless interment.

'I have a journal Miles was keeping,' I tell her. 'His, um, friends, I guess, gave it to me.'

'Rubbish, Bren.'

'You know what Caelyn has been studying, Mum. I know I told you it's all a bit out there, but I was wrong – and she's right. This stuff is really happening. I wouldn't say so if it wasn't true.'

She shakes her head sadly and picks up her bag. 'It's games night,' she says. 'We play Settlers of Catan and talk about how Jesus fed the fish, or something like that. I don't really pay attention.'

'Mum . . .'

'I don't know why you'd make up stories about something as serious as this. It's a horrible thing to do, love.' She kisses me on the cheek. 'Lock up when you go.' She leaves for church, and I raid the pantry for the biscuits I know are in there, somewhere.

—

Irving Shrike said *Voidstar* was a story without time, order or consequence. Things happened. It was, according to some, meaningless. I saw wonder, I think, in that meaninglessness, in those endless voids, in those shimmering pools of liquid sapphires, those cities, those civilisations; even in the collapses, the tiny defeats, the decayed fungi, the catastrophes. I used to think Miles saw things the same way. We were treading the same path. We would walk together, in some way, across seas, over mountains, in careers, through suburbs, through wars and disasters too, if they occurred. But he wasn't drawn to the same things at all. Maybe we were only treading the same path when there was no-one else around.

—

I flick to a page of the journal. There's a picture of a tree pasted on it: a redwood that has been cut out of a magazine. Next to it Miles had written: *I was born Californian. I'm not from here. I belong to the Pacific coast, the great redwood forests, the clear air. I'm not from here, but I can't walk away.*

On the opposing page he wrote about having a burger and coffee at an imagined roadside diner. He'd never been there but thought about it all the time.

I was pretty sure his parents were from Brisbane. Did he just want to go to California? Why? What was he trying to escape? Why couldn't he? There are too many unanswered questions, and this journal only raises new ones.

I close the journal and put it into a box. I drive to his old house. It's as it was years ago, if a little smaller, a little more decrepit. Standing on the footpath outside, I feel nothing but shame. I leave the small package on the front doorstep, and walk away.

—

I meet Mum for coffee in the morning at a beachside cafe next to an avenue of old Monterey cypresses. After a few quiet sips, she puts on her genuinely concerned face, touches my knee and asks, 'Do you have any close friends these days? I don't hear you talk about anyone much.'

'I have several acquaintances I can meet for coffee.'

'Yes, but you need close friends. People who understand you. People you can rely on.'

'I have Caelyn.'

'I mean other than your partner.'

'I have Travis.'

She rolls her eyes. 'I love your brother, but sometimes it feels like he only ever talks about what wine he wants you to buy from him next.'

'He's as close as I've got.'

She turns and looks out at the ocean. 'Yes. Well, I am glad you two get along at least. I worry about you, though. You never really did have close friends growing up, other than . . . you know.'

'Maybe I'm not the close friend type.'

She pats my knee. She sips her coffee, grimaces, and says, 'They made the coffee too cold again.'

—

Travis and I eat fish and chips on the beach we came to as kids. 'Remember when you climbed one of those?' he says, pointing to the tall Norfolk pines that line the foreshore.

'Yeah,' I say. I'd started climbing the tree and just kept going. Before I knew it, I was at the top, and it was a long way down.

I saw Dad waving at me to come down and Mum's hand on her heart. The wind was gentle, but cold. It was quiet up there. I don't remember how I got down again.

'Would you say you have any close friends?' I say.

'Nah,' he says. 'People just come and go. I like it like that. Let's go get some ice cream.'

Caelyn stares at her computer and doesn't say anything for a while. Then she lets out a huge sigh and closes her laptop. 'It's been accepted,' she says. 'No more rewrites.'

I say congratulations and hug her. She hugs back without enthusiasm. It's not what she'd wanted to write. They refused to acknowledge her evidence, using the excuse that she never sought ethics approval to test DNA. This is true, but approval wouldn't have been granted even if she had asked for it. A few of her colleagues suggested that her candidature be rescinded, but she clung on. She's been tenacious and adaptable. And brilliant.

'I'm taking you out,' I say. 'Let's drink some margaritas.'

She collapses onto the couch and weeps.

—

'Arrrggghhhhh!' she screams at the bar, surrounded by our friends and those few colleagues who'd remained supportive. 'Arrrrrgggghh!'

We laugh at first, but she does it a few too many times and things start to get uncomfortable.

Later, Caelyn and I sit on the disgusting sand of a city beach smoking a joint. The cool autumn evening is giving way to morning. We huddle close together to stay warm. There are a number of people around doing something similar. I ask her if she's happy and she says, 'This isn't happiness. It's something else.' She sucks the smoke in and releases it as if she's giving it to the sky. She coughs a few times. She doesn't really like smoking. 'Look up, Bren. You can see a few stars.'

—

She sends me a video of a news report about the growing number of missing people. The anchor crosses to a separate report about people standing around in the streets not moving.

'It's right in front of their eyes now,' Caelyn says. 'Why can't they see it?'

—

Conference rejections, postdoc rejections and no offers of teaching. Her supervisor doesn't attend her graduation. When her PhD title is announced – *Named Trees: A study of groups who believe in human-tree hybrids* – the crowd snickers.

She keeps applying for jobs. She keeps posting links to obscure articles and networking with like-minded people across the globe. She keeps writing, researching. She won't give up. But I don't know how much more rejection she can take. She's been quoting a lot of conspiracy theories. I'm worried she'll become one of those people who, after the world tells them no, follow increasingly tenuous threads until she becomes unrecognisable, becomes someone who looks up from their phone and no longer knows where they are, who is with them, and why they are here at all.

—

At the gym, I watch a video Travis sent me of a chat show. In their recurring segment 'Stuff We Didn't Need', one of the hosts says they've heard that someone wrote a PhD thesis about people turning into trees. The other hosts laugh. 'This is what our taxes pay for,' one of them says.

I mumble that there's not much government funding going to universities, so, no, your taxes didn't fucking pay for it.

The person on the next treadmill says, 'Huh?'

I say, 'Never mind.'

I don't tell Caelyn about the video. For a few days I'm tense, worried it will go viral. But it's not interesting enough to go viral. There's no dance associated with it, no pratfall or screaming creature. It's not punching down or up or casting aspersions. It holds little cultural weight. Besides, another queen has died. Not one of the popular queens but a different one, from a country that has several. It's enough to distract.

I watch Caelyn closely for a few days, observing her mood. It's normal; a little sullen, perhaps, but nothing too serious. At the end of the week, she insists we go out to the pancake house she used to visit as a kid, built to resemble something from the nineteenth century and where the staff wear top hats. I assume that means she's okay.

—

I'm called into the company's local headquarters, which is unusual because I didn't know it existed. They send a driverless taxi to pick me up, but I don't trust it. I take the train instead. The office is a single windowless room on the sixteenth floor of a very old building in the centre of the city. I assumed it would be glassy and breezy, an entire floor of people walking around with lots of natural light and free coffee. But it's an empty reception desk in front of a small room.

I knock on the door.

A deep, silky voice says, 'Yes, come in.'

I open the door to see a suave, silver-haired man in his fifties sitting behind a desk. He smiles with perfect teeth and says, 'Bren, it's good of you to come.' He shakes my hand. He smells like wood smoke and cedar. He's delightful.

'Bowden,' I say, 'nice to finally meet you. How long have we worked together now? Six years?'

He scratches his ear and says, 'Oh. Really?'

'Yes, I believe so.'

He shakes his head. 'No, I don't mean that. Never mind. Listen, um, Bren, we thought it was important to give you the news face to face. It is vital that we do human things together, don't you think?'

'Um, yes, sure.'

'The company is life-adjusting a number of positions given changing market circumstances. The Queue no longer requires authentic human interfaces.'

'Great,' I say.

'I am sorry,' Bowden says, and it looks like he genuinely means it.

—

I eat lunch in the cafe on the ground floor of the old office building. If I don't return home, I don't have to deal with the fact that I've lost my job. Not yet. I'm relieved. Is that the right way to feel in this situation? I don't know. So many years of the Queue. Did I accomplish anything? Does it matter? Who am I now? What might I become?

Why did I do this job for so long? It was meaningless. I knew it was meaningless. I spent much of my life working there. Does it matter? I was paid. Caelyn got through university. We've lived comfortably enough. But it meant nothing, and now it's done.

The Reuben sandwich I'm eating falls apart in my hands, but I stuff it all into my face anyway.

—

Bowden comes down to the cafe in the afternoon. I'm still there, on my third cup of coffee and second slice of cake. 'Can I sit?' he asks.

'There's no need to discuss anything,' I say. 'You made it perfectly clear.'

He sits anyway. 'No,' he says, shaking his head. 'I want to speak, um, off the record.'

'There's a record?'

He raises his eyebrows and nods. 'Oh, there's a record. Listen, you understand what I do, right?'

'You just fired me.'

'No, that's the thing . . .' To the waiter, he says, 'I'll have some tea thanks. Earl grey is fine.' Turning back to me, he continues, 'I'm not your manager.'

'You're not?'

'No. I'm an actor portraying your real manager. Everything up there was fed to me through an earpiece.'

'Who's my real manager?'

'I don't know. Someone who only wants to interact with people digitally. Someone who's got too much money and is very lazy. Or a non-human, I guess. Sure sounds like a non-human. Some alternative intelligence advanced enough to establish a personality and hold down a career. It doesn't matter. The point is this.' He hands me a card. It says: *Victor Hernandez, Senior Physical Relationship Agent, Cortexico Incorporated.*

'This is awful,' I say.

'You can earn a decent living,' he assures me. 'Maybe not as much as you made before, but still, a lot. Even with your, let's say, less striking look. You could afford to slouch less though. And skincare routines are a must.'

'It's awful, Bowden.'

'Victor.'

'Victor. It's still awful. I'm not sure I want to do things that are this awful.'

He smiles with his perfect teeth. 'Yeah. I wasn't sure either.'

—

Without my income, money quickly gets tight. Soon we're down to mostly buying packets of udon noodles, peanut butter and broccoli. Broccoli's expensive, though.

'I'm not giving up broccoli,' Caelyn says.

'There are challenging growth conditions,' I say.

'There are always challenging growth conditions.' She finishes her meal, rinses the plate, and puts it in the dishwasher. 'Doesn't stop things growing.' She looks around the apartment, full of plants and botanical drawings. 'Maybe I could go back to working at a nursery,' she says.

'Even though you were fired by one. Because you stole plants. Besides that, I'm still the one keeping these plants alive.'

She looks offended. 'How dare you,' she says. She flops down on the couch. 'Just because I have a professional interest in plants doesn't mean I'm able to care for them consistently. Do all psychologists have perfect mental health? Do all architects live in wonderful buildings?'

'Architects probably do.'

'Are doctors the healthiest people you know?'

'They're often quite healthy.'

'Whatever,' she says.

We spend a few hours watching a Spanish movie about a mean-spirited couple who lose their high-paying jobs due to a scandal and can't find other work. One of them dies of a drug overdose and the other ends up insane and starves to death in a ditch.

We don't sleep well.

Travis asks me what I'm going to do, and I say that I don't know what I'm going to do, and I'm about to talk about that some more when he says, 'Hey, have you tried last year's St Elias Estate riesling? It's a fucking banger. Citrus and plum and gooseberries and wet grass. Superb stuff.'

'I can't afford to buy your wine, Trav,' I say. 'Have you been listening?'

'Right, right. I could just use a few more sales of this one.'

'Is that how this works? You don't give recommendations, you just tell us about wines you need to move?'

'I only sell wines I recommend, Bren.'

—

The applications I send come back within minutes of submitting them. The responses are polite but uncompromising. Not the right experience; we had hundreds of excellent applications; it was a difficult decision; it's a competitive market and we're sure you'll end up where you need to be; your skills are no longer in demand; you're out of luck; we have no need of you; you are irrelevant; you have no worth; you do not belong; there is no capital that can be gained from your existence, you are, if anything, a drain on capital. They don't say that exactly, but I can read between the lines.

The applications Caelyn sends take days of work to compile, as she argues her case, updates her list of publications and responds to pages of questions. She never hears a word.

She says she thinks she made bad choices. I say if you hadn't made those choices, you'd wish you'd made those choices. She looks confused for a second, then agrees.

—

There's a spot on a hill that overlooks the city. We go there sometimes for the quiet. It's in a park frequented by cyclists and runners and bisected by the river. But this hill, crowned by Norfolk pines and not the usual gum trees, is off the track and not easy to find.

'I think society has very little use for my labour,' I say.

'That's nonsense,' Caelyn says. 'You're very useful.'

I hand her the bottle we brought.

'This isn't one of Travis's, is it?'

'Nup,' I say. 'We're on the ten-dollar shelf here. We're going to have preservative headaches tomorrow.'

She pours the wine into her cup and lies back on the grass, moving slightly to keep her freckled face in the shade. 'You're kind and smart. And funny.'

'I am funny,' I say. 'But I'm not smart. Or kind.'

'I've seen you be kind. To me. And to your mum. Sometimes Travis. Penny. Others, well, it takes a while for you to warm up to people.'

There's a wheel-whirr of cyclists on the road nearby. One of them loudly mentions selling his house, and then they're gone.

'All anyone ever talks about around here is real estate,' I say. 'How do you sell kindness?'

'You look after people.' She takes a sip and her eyes widen.

'Wine's good then?' I say.

She nods without speaking, making a show of trying to swallow. Eventually she does and rasps, 'It's time I gave up drinking.' She gently touches my shoulder, a gesture I never tire of. 'You could look after animals. Or plants. Or the earth. Or the sea. Or whales. Or –'

'Whales don't pay well.'

'We'll get through this,' she says.

'Yesterday you said you were giving up and going back to the country to grow vegetables.'

'Yet here I am today,' she says, 'not.'

'Not what?'

'Not giving up. Or moving back to the country.'

'Drinking cheap wine in the park seems pretty close to giving up.'

'No way,' she says. 'This is the opposite.'

As the sun sets, long shadows are cast by the hill and the pines on the city. We can almost see their edges if we look hard enough. There, shadow branches reach into an inner-city apartment building. There, on the ubiquitous hardware store. Slowly the city turns to gold, then pink, then neon orange. Blinking, flowing light, lives in comfortable boxes, pathways converging and diverging, the jumbled rivers and deltas of human existence. And next to me, her warmth, her smile, her calm. We clamber home drunkenly.

I sometimes remember how much I like the way she moves, but I see her move so often it's easy to forget.

—

I like to pretend sometimes that I can see my shadow on the moon's surface.

—

Caelyn publishes an article in a national news outlet and gets a few hundred dollars. It's mostly about why people choose to leave society to live in the tree communities she visits. She suggests, in passing, that she has found evidence of plant–animal hybridity in some of these communities, citing the paper she wrote with her geneticist friend Tomas, which was published in an obscure journal with a particularly low academic credibility rating. The editor of the news outlet positions the article as ludicrous clickbait. And yes, a few eyebrows are raised when it's published, but most of the comments are written by people whose family or friends have left to go to these communities. There are a few comments from people in Scotland, Mexico and India who say they have seen people turn into trees several times. The editor says he's happy with the response to the article, but Caelyn knows he's not. 'He wanted me to be humiliated,' she says.

'You showed him,' I say. 'Barely got any clicks at all.'

She kicks me gently with her foot and Henry leaps out of my lap and scurries to the bedroom.

—

The way I bob on the surface, not drowning but drifting; the way she swims furiously for the islands she can see in the distance.

—

We float together for three months, unemployed, unsure. I lose all confidence, she loses some, gains it back, loses it again.

We're almost out of money when she gets a message from Arlene. She hasn't seen Arlene since Italy. She's working for the University of Edinburgh, doing research with the Royal Botanic Garden. She says a few of her colleagues read Caelyn's article and they'd like to talk to her. Caelyn calls them. They reveal that they've seen footage of a few people who hid themselves away in the gardens over the last few weeks. There's nothing there now but a few elm trees that weren't there before. They wonder if she would be interested in a postdoctoral position.

She would be, yes. We pack up our apartment, end the lease, and leave Henry with Mum. She's happy to have the company. Morgan's upset, but Caelyn says it's mostly because she's down a babysitter. Her dad says he's proud, and her mum sniffs that it's not exactly Cambridge. Travis gives us a bottle of not-quite-top-shelf pinot noir, and I say we can't really take that with us, and he says, of course, of course, and happily takes it back.

She's a confident swimmer. It was just a matter of finding the wave that would carry her to shore. And I'm there, hanging on beside her as we come into land at Edinburgh Airport.

—

Life speeds up.

Caelyn joins a small team of researchers at the university, and she's soon publishing papers, lecturing, and presenting at conferences. I freelance when I can find the work, and often accompany her on trips around Europe to investigate sightings of people becoming trees. We travel most weekends, devouring new places and new ideas. We are busy, light-filled, and happy.

Videos of the struggles of people digging in become so numerous it's impossible to call it all fake. An Oscar winner is witnessed becoming an alder tree in Beverly Hills, setting off a media frenzy. Within a year, people around the world begin to understand. What was a trickle becomes a flood. The evidence that people demanded is everywhere. All over the planet, people are becoming trees. Previously secretive communities come out of hiding, emboldened.

Caelyn is soon given a tenured position, and quickly promoted. She publishes a book called *Arborescence*, in which she writes compellingly about the development of human-plant hybridity, the tree communities she's encountered, the myths that they are cult-like or profoundly spiritual, and the increasing prevalence of the phenomenon in the wider community. Her conclusion is that while we should try to understand it more than we do, arborescence shouldn't be feared. The book is compassionate and fascinating, and published at the right time. She is interviewed by the BBC about human-tree hybridity. People are looking for answers, or at least a voice of calm. She's nervous at first, but soon it's as if she's been doing it for years.

She visits communities across Europe, researching, talking, reassuring.

She teaches until she is so busy she can't teach anymore. Offers to speak come in from across the world.

In some of the more disturbed corners of the internet, she's even spoken of as a prophet.

This is, she admits, a change in her fortunes, and one that she doesn't feel she deserves. Right place at the right time, she says, but it doesn't feel like the right place or the right time to me at all.

4

Arthur's Seat, visible from the window of our fourth-floor flat, is no longer as treeless as it was when we arrived five years earlier. Small copses are scattered on it. Sometimes, while I'm organising Caelyn's calendar, I watch people walking up it, eventually stopping somewhere they deem worthy and standing still. Sometimes they're being funny and leave after a few minutes. Sometimes they stay there for days. Sometimes they become a tree. This, many locals say, cannot continue. Arthur's Seat was bald for a reason. But who's going to cut them down?

—

Driving to a conference in another city, we pass a rabbit sitting in the middle of the road. It's alive and uninjured, but frozen in place as cars hurtle past. The rabbit has buried its face in its paws, as if to shield it from its inevitable doom.

'It's almost human,' I say. 'Can we go back and save it?'
Caelyn says that we would just be killed too in the attempt.
'But we can't just leave it there,' I say. 'Poor little guy.'
'It's probably already dead,' she says. 'They're pests anyway.'
'I'm not sure they're pests here,' I say.

'We used to hit four or five of them a night when I was growing up. It happens. There's so many of them. You just have to keep going.'

'But did you see the way it buried its face in its paws? It's like it was saying, *I don't want to die. I just want to be safe in my home with my family*, or whatever.'

'Why does something seeming human make you more inclined to save it?' she says.

'I'm just not sure I'll be able to get that image out of my head,' I say.

—

I've heard that the ruins of the old city are spectacular. But when I visit, I realise that the new city is just as ruined. It was a war, perhaps, or natural decay and economic rot. There are holes in the road, children with blank expressions, collapsed apartment buildings, twisted girders grasping at the sky. A few tall trees rise from the ruins, but not many.

I hurry back to the conference centre and watch Caelyn's presentation from a quiet corner. She prefers me not to come to her lectures. She says I distract her.

She prowls the stage, poking and provoking and making jokes. She has the crowd in the palm of her hand. They're almost reverential. She looks in my direction, hesitates briefly, narrows her eyes and continues. She says, 'But to answer your question, no. Arborescent individuals are not suicidal. They instead seek to extend their lives without unbalancing the planet further.'

She pauses for effect. She's become an expert at these presentations. She still gets nervous. But when she's up there, she's extraordinary. Funny, interesting, impossible not to watch. She wears expensive suits and has her hair done properly. These days, we even have Travis's wine shipped over sometimes.

'It often becomes their perspective,' she says, her voice becoming sharp and rising in volume, 'that muscle-bound, kinetically cursed creatures damage everything they touch. We destroy. We take and we do not give. We consume until there is nothing left. We dig and scratch and stomp and kill and cut and burn.'

She pauses again, as if she herself has just felled a tree with an axe. She takes a deep breath. The audience is silent. The light in the auditorium becomes a green-yellow, the colour of sun-dappled forest. The lightest sound of a string quartet can be heard. She invites local musicians to play in every city she visits.

'But trees,' she says, more softly now, 'are the highest form of life. Life that gives, that connects, that is at peace with its place and does not seek to change it, does not want beyond what it needs, does not take, does not destroy.'

Another pause. This question has been asked before, by people suffering the loss of loved ones. She has answered it many times, kindly. But she has no need to pause or think about it. It's all for effect.

'Our arborescent friends and family aren't suicidal. They don't have much faith in humanity, perhaps' – the audience laughs, and she lets them – 'and maybe not in God, however you construct

Them. But they have faith. In earth, in the sun, in the wind and in the clouds. But you want a more personal take. We all do. We all want answers. It's hard to believe that we're here, isn't it? That so much has changed in only a few years? That our co-workers, parents, friends have planted themselves near a river, or on the outskirts of town, or even on the street itself? We all know one, don't we?'

She pauses again.

'But let's try to think of it like this. What they are saying, what each one of them is saying when they decide to dig in, to stand exposed to the sun and the rain and the earth, is this.' She clasps her hands together and looks out at the audience earnestly. 'All is not lost, friends. All is not lost.'

The lights in the auditorium take on an effect of golden stars or spores, shimmering, dancing and falling in sunlight. I hear a few gasps and a few sobs. Then, a standing ovation. She smiles, bows, thanks them and walks off the stage.

Mostly they are old, or toward the end of their lives. That makes sense to people. A life lived fully, followed by another. It is, in a sense, selfish. A chance at something more. But it's the ones who arboresce in the prime of their lives, or, worse, the children, that concern people the most. All that squandered human potential; all those delicate saplings waving in the breeze.

—

Travis visits us in Scotland for a while and tries to establish a business. But within a few months he meets Shakti. They marry in India, move back to Australia and have a child – all in the space of a year. Mum joins several book clubs at once, spoils Henry and calls often to tell me what she's worried about. Caelyn takes her parents on a tour of the English and Scottish countryside and swears, after they've gone home, to never do it again. She calls Morgan and Penny every week, and often watches Penny play football over video calls, at times shouting, 'Ball!' a little too loudly for our neighbours.

I work in bookstores, in bars. I create a video game about sentient blocks of concrete that makes enough for a few pub meals. But we have more money than we need. As Caelyn's workload has grown, more of my time has been devoted to supporting her. I make sure she eats well, that her clothes are drycleaned. I book her flights and find her suitable hotels. I manage her schedule so that she has enough time to write her columns and do her research between the public speaking, the interviews and the forums. I organise for her to visit local communities. I edit her work and email publicists on her behalf. I take photographs and notes. I don't spend as much time with her as I'd like. She needs space to work, so I walk around cities and villages, looking for ruins. I'm not interested in monuments or galleries. I'm not interested in what people have created. It's more comforting to explore what has fallen down.

I am her assistant and her confidant. When people ask me what I do, I say that she needs an administrator. On the off chance that this isn't enough for them, I say that I believe her work is more important than anything I could contribute. She's brilliant and restless, spiky and witty, full of energy but always tired.

At the end of the day, she collapses into bed beside me and falls asleep immediately. She has changed beyond anything we could have imagined, but I think I've stayed the same.

—

We are, very slowly, falling out of each other's orbit.

—

I keep thinking about the rabbit.

A woman introduces herself at a book signing. She's in her sixties, appears malnourished, and vaguely familiar. She and Caelyn talk and exchange details. The woman leaves, and Caelyn looks at me and mouths, 'Vera Parkes!' I shrug indifferently and she rolls her eyes and greets the next person in the queue.

Caelyn constantly complained about Vera Parkes during her doctorate. She's a controversial Canadian academic who has for years espoused the need for humans to live more like trees. While initially harmless, her ideas have become increasingly unhinged. She only eats food that theoretically might have been able to escape. She believes that the human population is due an enormous correction. She once suggested that humans shouldn't talk, that they should be as quiet as trees, but has since abandoned that position as it became less convenient and now pretends she never said it. These days she claims that arborescence was what she was talking about all along. That she predicted it. It's clear she courts controversy and attention and will assume any position that ensures her own relevance.

Caelyn joins me after the signing and says excitedly, 'Vera Parkes just told me she loves my work!'

'You refused to use her research when you were writing your PhD. You said it was pseudoscience.'

She waves me away. 'People change,' she says.

'You said she was a nutcase.'

'She's unconventional, sure, but maybe that's our problem, not hers. Maybe we've been too conventional for too long. Maybe we need to abandon convention.'

'Are you only going to eat roadkill now or something?'

'I'm just happy she acknowledged me.' She walks off, then turns and says, 'She eats roadkill?'

—

'If I could fix this,' she says, four tequila shots down in a New York City bar, 'I'm not sure I would.' We all stare at the trees scattered in inconvenient places on the pavement outside. 'I think it's quite lovely.'

'But you can't fix it,' Margaret says.

'No,' Caelyn says.

'But if you could,' I say.

'You wouldn't,' Ada says.

Caelyn says, 'It's not something we need to fix.'

'Hmph,' Ada says, and Caelyn says she loves New Order and the bartender turns it up.

We stop talking for a while. Outside I see a woman sit with a dogwood tree in the middle of the road. Cars drive around it as if it's a roundabout. The woman rests in its thick roots and talks to it.

'It feels like something that needs fixing,' I say.

Caelyn frowns. 'You think this is worse than what we had before?'

Ada says, 'No, I agree with Bren – this is super fucked up, Caelyn. We're losing so many people.'

'This isn't losing,' Caelyn says. 'We're not losing. We're just changing.'

'Ugh,' Margaret says. 'You're sounding like Vera Parkes.'

I exchange a look with Caelyn, who looks to see if I am exchanging a look with her. When she finds that I am, her gaze goes back to her drink. This morning I told her that, up until very recently, Parkes tried to make the small British Columbian island she owns a sovereign state.

Ada says, 'At least we're all still human, hey?' and raises her drink for a toast.

We clink our glasses together.

Caelyn drinks and adds, 'For now! But next year, who knows?'

They laugh and I do too, but I'm not sure how convincing I sound.

—

The news report declares that the speed at which people are becoming trees is alarming. From hundreds, to thousands, to millions. Some experts believe we're running out of time; that within a few years we'll be gone completely. Caelyn is quoted as saying she doesn't agree, but that it beats dying from climate change. On the screen in our hotel room, we watch her face crack a wry smile. I look over at her on the couch and she shrugs, cracking the same wry smile as she watches herself.

—

At the hotel in the new Saudi Arabian metro-structure (calling it a city is both underselling and overselling it), I spy a copy of one of Vera Parkes' recently published novels in Caelyn's bag. She returns from her swim and joins me on the balcony. 'I can't believe they actually built something like this,' she says. 'It's as if we're finally saying we're not of this earth. We're something else.'

'The panel went well then.'

'They see it as a mental illness,' she says. 'So few that dig in here arboresce fully. The climate is so hostile. But there are just as many trying as anywhere else. They just aren't making it. The official position is that it's all in people's heads, despite the mountains of evidence to the contrary. The moderator was careful to say that there are of course two sides to every story, and that Western thought paradigms are not always compatible with Arabian. I was going to argue, but the guy gave me this panicked look. I don't think I want to come here again.'

'Okay,' I say, giving her some iced water. 'I'll cancel any future visits.'

'Thanks.'

'How's the Vera Parkes book coming along?'

She snaps me a look. 'It's surprisingly funny. It's a loosely fictionalised biography of a woman who is unfairly hounded out of academia because she believes in the purity of flowers and the staged removal of humans from the earth. She makes some good points.'

'Caelyn,' I say, 'I've done a bit of research.'

'Ooh,' she says. 'I love research.'

'She was suspended from her tenured position because she was a liar, incompetent and repeatedly purported to be an expert in subjects that were far from her area of expertise. Why would you read her stuff? Aren't you interested in facts? In truth?'

'She has interesting things to say. And do you mind not going through my bag?'

'The book fell out when I picked it up. And she's an extremist who would be quite happy if humanity was extinguished tomorrow.'

She waves me away. 'That's just talk,' she says.

'If she's so into trees, why hasn't she become one herself?'

'Not everyone has the capacity.'

'Bullshit. She just doesn't want to. She's normalising this stuff, declaring that everyone should be fine with losing people to a Douglas fir or whatever, and meanwhile she's just waiting it out on her island.'

I go to stand at the balcony railing and watch the plaza below. It is decorated beautifully with swinging lights, pavilions, flowers and plants that have been manicured into alien shapes. But it seems almost abandoned. A lone man crosses from one glassy building to the next. There's no-one else around. A stream of drones fly above, delivering, watching, washing windows and streets, monitoring. Probably scheming.

Caelyn joins me and puts her arms around my waist.

'Look at this place,' she whispers in my ear. 'This is the best we can do. This.' She makes a grand gesture at the glass, the concrete, the drones and the steel. 'Don't you think she might have a point?'

I gently push her away. 'No,' I say. 'I don't.'

Voidstar #34: The Lightless Dirge. The young creature asks Voidstar, currently a formless collection of rays of light, why they're called Voidstar. The rays of light shift and shimmer, casting their beams over the rock and sand and sky. When the answer comes, it conveys – according to the iconic images in the issue illustrated by Renee Kuip – several answers at once. It suggests that language is either an empty vessel, or an archaic concept used by gas breathers to assert meaning where there is none, or an ugly orchid on a quiet, rain-soaked moor, or one of hundreds of other images. David Bowie and Grace Jones feature in one. There's what appears to be a black hole. A brazier being lit by a flaming torch. A bearded human sitting at a drawing board holding a pen. A spinning array of stars. A village floating over a waterfall. A space station shaped like a corkscrew, spinning over a gas giant, where thousands of ships arrive and leave. A book, opened at a page that says, *So it goes.* And so on, and so on. The young creature is enthralled. Its eyes go black, and it returns to its caregiver, who asks where the young creature has been. The young creature cannot answer. It has become catatonic. The caregiver becomes furious and tells other creatures. They have a long, angry discussion, and blame Voidstar for what has happened to the young one. The creatures try to destroy Voidstar. They use every weapon they have: energy projectors, fire, flying metal. Voidstar doesn't move and doesn't respond. They're just light, after all. The creatures eventually give up. Years go by. Creatures die and are recycled. After fifty orbits of the star engine, the once-young creature finally wakes. Its eyes focus. Now, in its last years, the creature tracks Voidstar down. They are in the same place they were when they last met, fifty star turns ago. The creature sits next to the shimmering rays of light and doesn't say anything for a while. After some time it says, 'Thank you, but you didn't answer the question.'

In a community in Montreal, fifteen people die after trying to dig in too close to winter. Some of them had already taken root, some were in that grotesque halfway stage somewhere between person and tree. We arrive as they are being carefully removed. Caelyn tells me to take pictures, but I don't really want to.

—

'You are flying around the world,' says the grumpy Québécois. 'Why do you need to fly around the world to say these things?'

A few members of the audience clap.

For a moment Caelyn is thrown. I can see it in her face, a subtle tension that is gone almost as soon as it arrives. 'I took the train from New York here, actually,' she says. 'But yes, sometimes flights are necessary. I minimise them when I can.'

'You are part of the problem!' the Québécois shouts.

More heckles follow.

She raises her hands in a pacifying gesture. 'Yes,' she says, 'I am. And so are you. By merely existing, you have disturbed the planet. You are part of the great tide of humanity that has tipped the balance. We're all the problem, my friend.'

There are some more mutterings, and she lowers her hands and puts on her earnest face.

'I know this is scary. I know it doesn't make a lot of sense. I've lost friends to it too. And I know people are saying that it's related to human activity. We have no scientific evidence of that. But I do think that arborescence is telling us that humanity needs to change. We've been winning for a long time. Maybe we need to lose for a while.'

'You know nothing about loss!' the man screams.

—

The bar shines with Parisian flair, but last I checked we were in Slovakia. The Frenchman beside me has been talking about gestalt consciousnesses, but at me, not with me. I may as well not be here. I tell him I don't care about AI, but he tells me I do, and continues explaining why it doesn't need us anymore. Eventually he discovers that Caelyn is my partner and he looks at me as if seeing me for the first time. The presence of fame, however indirect, focuses people. They sense opportunity. But all he says is, 'She is a light in the dark.' He raises his glass and toasts her.

'I'm glad you think so,' I say.

He looks at me with a stupid smile, as if I've made his day, then finishes his drink, makes some excuse about family and leaves.

—

'What do you do?' the Swedish academic asks.

Caelyn puts her hand on my arm and says, 'He works with robots.'

It's an old joke, but it irritates me.

'I was a Queue Curator.'

The man's moustache is thin and irritating. He twirls its ends constantly, as if he wants it to be noticed. He's an expert on the psychology of digital media. He says, 'Ah, I see.'

'Now he's my assistant,' Caelyn says.

'Manager,' I say.

'Sure,' she says, smiling.

'Hmm,' he says. 'Interesting.'

'I think we're out of wine,' I say.

—

'Every time I want to understand irony, I have to look it up,' I say. 'Then I understand it again and I think, oh, this is irony, and then I immediately forget the definition until something else looks ironic. Then I have to go and look it up again. It's like my brain refuses to absorb it. I've learned so many things over the years, but my brain will not let me absorb that one. Is that ironic? I have no idea.'

'I'll have the pasta,' she says to the waiter. When he leaves, she rests her cheek on her hand and says, 'I just want a sandwich.'

—

An overseas war unfolds on a screen in our Los Angeles hotel room. The possibility that mass arborescence might calm us down as a species has not yet played out.

The Californian arborescence phenomenon is one of the world's largest. A few hours ago, Caelyn explained to a packed audience the theory that there is a psychological aspect to those who arboresce.

'It is something that must be done willingly,' she told them. 'It cannot be forced. California has one of the highest rates of arborescence, as you know. There are many reasons why that might be the case. We have considered that it might be a response to stress, but if anything, pre-arborescent individuals show signs of optimism rather than pessimism, and no correlation has been found between stress and arborescent tendencies. The research, like all research into arborescence, is still in its infancy.'

'This has been happening for years,' a woman cried out, 'and the research is just starting? What have you scientists been doing all this time?'

Caelyn's publicist looked around nervously.

Caelyn said, 'We're all working hard to understand this problem. It is, however, a problem that is very hard to understand. Many of the models we have simply don't work. We're doing our best.'

The crowd grumbled, but she held on to them. Early on, when she was still teaching at the university, her audiences were appreciative. This was probably because arborescence was happening to other people. But the crowds have become much more tense as the problem has become worse.

On the screen in the hotel room, a missile is flung violently from a large ground device. We haven't moved far from catapults and trebuchets, except now we can kill across many, many kilometres, without the killers having to see the results of their work.

Caelyn says, 'Plants don't have borders.'

'Surely the limits of their roots and branches are a border,' I say.

She looks at me wearily and doesn't answer. She's been doing that a lot lately. She goes for a swim.

—

This all happened to her so quickly. It was a thrill, at first, to be along for the ride. I'm just not sure how much longer I want to be a tourist.

—

We used to meet mutual friends for dinner sometimes, but now, when we travel, we only meet Caelyn's colleagues. These colleagues are like friends but not friendly. They like to poke holes in her arguments and undermine her position. She enjoys it. She bites back, hard; delights in pricking their bubbles with her pins; loves watching them stumble and fall. And then she sinks her teeth in, shakes them to make sure they're dead. Sometimes I swear she sets them up just so she can tear them down.

They are so consistently bemused by my presence I'm becoming bemused by it myself.

—

We live in hotel rooms where the plants never die.

—

At the conference in Geneva, the young professor says that animals were invented by plants, so who's to say they can't uninvent us?

'You've been reading too much Terence McKenna,' the other professor says. 'You know, he predicted the world would end in 2012.'

'What,' the young professor says, 'you don't think it did?'

—

'Plants and animals are not symbiotes, not in the true sense of the word,' the Tanzanian academic says to Caelyn.

We are standing on the wide balcony of a conference centre that overlooks a huge, chaotic botanic garden.

Caelyn says that our taxonomies are hopelessly inadequate.

I consider the tray of small quiches carefully.

—

'Are romantic relationships symbiotic?' I ask that night. She lies down in bed and covers her head with blankets.

'No,' she says. 'Symbiosis takes a few forms. Parasitic, mutualist, commensalistic, amensalistic. Nothing like us. We are just two humans floating in space, occasionally keeping each other warm.'

'I feel a bit parasitic,' I say.

She laughs under the covers and says, 'Prague is always so cold when I'm here. I wish they'd invite me in summer. Could you give me your legs?'

ARBORESCENCE

—

Skin taking on the form of lichen could be a case of bad hygiene, or something more serious. I moisturise more than I used to.

—

'So they've established it's not transmissible,' I say on the transcontinental train. 'But what if it isn't a natural phenomenon at all? What if it's been cooked up in some lab? What if it's biological warfare?'

'Pretty imprecise weapon,' Caelyn says.

Mountains and fields fly past; people in tiny villages watch on. Trees in the middle of fields, trees in the water, trees emerging from ruins.

'Depends who your enemies are,' I say.

She slouches in her seat and closes her eyes. 'I don't think anyone could make this happen if they wanted to,' she says. 'I think what it means to be human might be changing. Maybe just in time.'

—

On a street corner near a diner, four homeless men stand still, facing the sun. A police car arrives. The officers get out and wave the men on. They don't move. A few more words are exchanged, accompanied by emphatic gestures. One officer yells, 'There's no planting here, sir. Let's get a move on.'

No-one moves.

An officer shoves one gently and he falls over. Then he shoves another, who also falls over, and another. The last doesn't budge. The officer looks at the man's feet and swears. 'We'll need a removal crew for this one,' he says.

Laughter. The three other men stand unsteadily and shuffle away.

Mum hasn't been calling as much, so I've been calling her. She used to worry all the time. About the bees, the pigs in the farms, the ducks, the cows, the kids with all the online stuff, whether she should wear what she was going to wear. She's quieter now. It's hard to say if she still worries. I call her from a bar in Chicago.

'How are you doing, love?' she says.

'I'm fine,' I say. 'How are you?'

'I'm fine.' She takes a long breath. 'The man over the road died last night.'

'Oh,' I say, 'I'm sorry to hear that.'

'I never knew his name,' she says. 'What sort of a world do we live in where I don't even know the name of one of my oldest neighbours? We've both lived here for years; we even said hello to each other sometimes.'

'It's a strange time,' I say.

'It's not that strange,' she says. 'It's always been like this. We just haven't noticed it. Where are you?'

'Chicago.'

'How's Caelyn?'

'Tired,' I say.

'She's always on the news.'

'Yeah.'

'I've got some gardening to do,' she says, 'then I'm going to pop down and see Dad.'

'Right. Um, say hello.'

'Love, you can't talk to the dead.'

'Before you go,' I say, 'how are the bees doing?'

'Ugh,' she says, 'what's the point in worrying about bees when we're all just bees?'

'I'm not sure I understand that, Mum.'

'No, well, I'm on some new medication. Makes things a little bendy. Off I trot. Bye, love.'

'Wait,' I say, but she hangs up. I look around at the bar, full of life and subtle lighting and people who know a lot about baseball. I don't know why I'm here.

—

In Florida there's a small cypress forest overrun with Spanish moss. Some local academics are excited to show Caelyn. They say it's something she hasn't seen before. She humours them, but she and I exchange sceptical looks.

It's a swampy, marshy, bedraggled landscape, infested with alligators and snakes that swim and other things I have no interest in meeting. After half an hour of skimming through the Everglades on an airboat, we spy a small island cluttered with pick-up trucks, each embedded in the thick trunk of a cypress. If these trees were once people, they must have stood on the trays for weeks until their roots broke through or grew around the trucks. Some of the bigger trees have trucks embedded several metres off the ground.

We disembark and I start taking photos while Caelyn makes notes.

'See?' one of the academics says. 'This is something new. These people grew into a forest based on a shared interest.'

Caelyn says, 'The Nürburgring in Germany is covered with so many trees the cars can no longer race there. They had to move matches from the Bernabéu because of the trees in the stands. There's nothing new about this. How'd they get their trucks out here?'

'A barge,' one of them says, pointing to the nearby dock.

Caelyn makes some more notes. 'We see this a lot,' she says. 'Some people hope to find new family in arborescence. I'm not convinced it works that way. Visually impressive, though, don't you think?' She nudges me. 'Some good images would be great for the socials.'

I agree and take a photo of a rusted Ford F-150, half crushed by the strength of its host.

'Do you think these people were trying to make a point about nature overcoming human invention?' I say.

'They probably just liked trucks,' she says.

—

Caelyn says we can't use any of the photos from the island. I took three hundred and none of them work. I don't know why. It's something about the framing, or the lighting, or something she's looking for that she can't express. She says she'll hire a professional photographer next time. By which she means I will hire a photographer; she hasn't hired anything herself for years.

—

I rarely see Caelyn between speaking engagements. She doesn't attend the university that employs her. They demanded she teach a class this semester, but she refused, and they won't press her. She's on their billboards, website and promotional videos, even though she didn't authorise it. I've stopped going to the dinners and the drinks and most of the sessions. I alternate between sitting in hotel rooms and walking the streets of cities I don't know, looking at the increasing number of abandoned buildings. The streets themselves are often quiet, except for the buzzing of drones.

—

Online: which singer has planted themselves in which ex's yard, what fertilisers are good for relatives, can drinking ionised water prevent arborescence, how can I decolonise my digging in, is poisoning a tree murder, is it cheating if I slept with my girlfriend's best friend after my girlfriend became a tree, and on and on.

—

There's a new by-law in San Francisco that prohibits the planting of oneself on city property. The by-law hasn't stopped people from occupying parks, cemeteries or the pavement outside the local Starbucks. *Cut this asshole down*, the police say. Although the cutting isn't always cutting. It depends on where the tree is at in its life cycle.

Caelyn and her colleagues have identified three stages of arborescence. The first is the kinetic, in which the human is more human than tree, and the roots have barely begun to take. The nervous system still functions, slightly, and blood still flows through the cardiovascular system. The individual requires more water but is usually unable to indicate that they do. Bones and muscles start to harden, making it easier for the nascent arborescent to stand upright over the weeks to come. Light photosynthesis begins, and the skin takes on a greenish tinge. The eyes, if they are open, often contain flecks of gold-green. Nutrients begin to be absorbed through the feet.

The second stage is called the dormant-transitory. Human systems mostly cease, but photosynthesis has not completely taken hold. The skin thickens and small branches and leaves may begin to form. It's a halfway state. The being doesn't appear alive but nor do they appear dead. No blood flows, no respiration occurs. The occasional sound can be heard coming from the mouth. As it progresses, bark begins to form on the skin. It is said to be extraordinarily painful, but no-one has returned from this state to confirm that. The nervous system often continues functioning for some time, suggesting the individual remains aware of their surroundings, and tests have suggested a response to pain. It is the most dangerous stage, when almost all failures occur: the individual either transforms or dies.

The final stage is called the arborescent. Following the shut down of the last remaining human system, the roots dig deep, far more quickly than a tree naturally would. In some cases, the roots break through concrete in a matter of hours. The trunk grows high and thick around the individual, so that there is rarely a trace of the human left. (Very occasionally, due to the lava-like way the tree both absorbs and grows over the human, there might be a spare tooth or a limb jutting out from the bark.) It's hard to say by looking at it whether a tree was formerly human or not. You can only tell by association – by the people who show up to put flowers at its feet, or by the locations they choose to dig in: a favourite cafe, a beautiful vista, a family home, the middle of the street.

In certain jurisdictions, trees are removed. It is a contentious topic, akin to human execution in the eyes of some. The method depends on the stage. A form that is still kinetic can be gently uprooted and, if caught early enough, can sometimes be rehabilitated to human form. An arborescent form is effectively a tree, and – although the sight of what remains of the human embedded in its trunk can be confronting – it may be cut down or removed in the traditional way. The most difficult to deal with are those in the dormant-transitory stage. No matter how they are removed, they scream, bleed and gush. Most governments prefer to avoid this. In many US cities, patrols scout the streets looking for kinetics to move in order to prevent progression to the second form. Lately, it's only been taking a few days to transition from stage one to stage two. Loitering is prohibited. If you're not moving, you're a criminal.

Caelyn says that people are scared, but really, there's nothing to fear.

'I don't know,' I say. 'It seems pretty fucking scary to me.'

—

'I tried once,' she says. We're in a short-stay apartment in Madrid while she appears at several events. 'Back in Edinburgh. Supervised of course. Arlene's team was ready to shake me out of it the moment they saw a green tinge to the skin. But it never took.'

I place the plate I'm drying on the counter. 'You tried? Why would you try?'

'We were doing some tests. But it never took. And I really, really tried. I don't know what's wrong with me. It seems so easy for everyone else. I mean, I'm glad. It's revolting, really.'

I don't know what to do with this revelation, so I stay silent and bang the remaining plates as loudly as I can without breaking them.

—

A man at the coffee shop in Boston tells another that Maurice waited until Alan went on holiday then planted himself in his neighbour's driveway. The other man laughs and says, 'What type?' The first man says, 'A birch.' The other man laughs and says, 'A fucking birch. What's Alan going to do?' The first man says, 'Ah, man, Maurice knew Alan wouldn't cut him down.

He sold up and moved to Florida.' The other man doubles over laughing. 'Fucking Alan,' he says.

—

In Buenos Aires we watch a crowd attempt to become a sanctioned urban park. Their families and friends hold vigils, and there's nothing of the usual police presence or protest that has occurred in other areas of the world. Our hotel overlooks the scene. We watch for a few weeks as the transformation takes place. Caelyn gives a rousing speech to the assembled supporters, telling them that these heroes are doing a great and noble thing. People cheer, even as they are losing their loved ones permanently.

I've stopped talking to Caelyn about how disturbed I am. In the night she sleeps soundly, while I lie awake listening to the low wooden-throated groans of people in the last, painful throes of arborescence.

They are becoming jacarandas, they say, like the rows of jacarandas that line the city's streets, covering Buenos Aires with purple flowers in spring. Caelyn says it's a lovely intention but offers no more than that. We leave before they're finished, and for a while I don't hear any more about them.

—

'This is how we take control of the planet from ourselves,' she says, and although that's a confusing statement, the audience in Singapore gives her a standing ovation. Outside the auditorium they're selling t-shirts and nutritional supplements.

We have a heated argument about a scheduling mix-up that becomes about everything other than the schedule. She says that I need to find a purpose, and I tell her that despite her public persona she doesn't believe in anything, only the things that get her the most attention. This is only partially true, but sometimes you say things to make things happen, even if they're only partially true. She goes for dinner alone and we don't talk for three days.

—

I see an email from Vera Parkes while I'm organising Caelyn's calendar. It says:

> Love your work, Caelyn. The movement is growing, and much of it is thanks to you and your efforts. Come up to BC sometime and visit. Morton and I would love to have you.

—

'Is this a movement?' I say. 'Is there some nefarious organisation behind all of this?'

'What? A movement? No,' Caelyn says. 'Sometimes people like to give others the impression they're in control. Sometimes movements form after the fact. Do you think they do cinnamon rolls here?'

'You could ask,' I say.

She looks at her laptop and then at me.

I say, 'I'll go and ask.'

—

It's spring in Buenos Aires and I watch a video of a park full of blooming jacarandas, their purple flowers a carpet, the roots of the trees cracking the concrete.

—

We live in hotels and we live like we are not the problem.

—

Book signings, research seminars, conferences, sold-out panels, interviews.

This is good for us, she tells every audience. She explains what researchers understand about arborescence. She explains why there's nothing to fear. It isn't an end, it's a beginning. She is calm, and she is funny, and she is empathetic, and yet, I think, there is something very, very wrong with her. I think she's enjoying what is happening to us.

—

'You're seriously going to stay with Vera Parkes on her sovereign island?' I ask.

'Are you reading my emails?' Caelyn responds.

'Of course I am. You gave me your passwords. How else do you think I'm supposed to work out where you're supposed to be?'

She throws clothes into her suitcase.

'I'd normally fold those up or they'll crease,' I say.

She stops and puts her hand on her forehead. 'Bren,' she says, 'yes: I'm going to stay with Vera. She has important things to say. She's a pioneer.'

'You agree with her that the world needs fewer humans and more trees.'

'Don't you?'

'On a conceptual level, yes, but not on the level she advocates. A few years ago she wrote about killing people, knocking down their houses and planting trees where they lived.'

'That was taken out of context,' she says.

'Caelyn, can't you see where this is going?'

She throws her shoes into the bag. 'I can see,' she says, her voice shaking now, 'that the world is sick, that it is deeply, deeply sick, and while we have caused it there is nothing our stupid meat brains can do to fix it. We can't control ourselves, our greed, our urges. We can sit around like this, talking about reductions and degrowth and rewilding and all that bullshit, but it comes down to the fact that humans hoard and consume far more than we need just to make life slightly easier for ourselves. We will never give up anything, not really, unless we're forced to. And I can see, Bren, that trees do not do this. And I can see,' she says, pushing one of her shoes awkwardly into the bottom of the bag, 'that this condition I am allegedly an authority on – despite not knowing what has caused it or how to fix it – is actually a bloody good thing. And if I can help by easing people's minds, by showing them that it is the right thing, it will be easier for us all. Better than death by blood and war and heat and drowning and starvation, don't you think?'

I look at her. She stops packing for a moment and looks back at me. She has her hand on her hip. We've looked at each other so often for so many years. But she's not the person I knew. She's grown and twisted, the way trees sometimes do in response to something obstructing their growth. She's still there, but she's not the same.

I'm not sure I believe in her.

'You're a hypocrite,' I say.

'Oh, am I? Then what the fuck are you?'

'I believe that people are good, and worth saving. Yes: we're worth saving. We're broken, but we're incredible. You, you're advocating for balance by telling us all to jump off a cliff.'

She frowns. 'That's not what this –'

I hold up my hands. 'Allow the metaphor.' It happens all at once, a flood of words, years of not saying them. I can't stop them. 'You're telling people they should all become trees because that will save the planet. But you have no intention of doing the same. You're saying to them, "All is not lost," but like that Canadian said, you've suffered no real loss yourself. You don't know what they're going through and neither do I. You're a hypocrite. Just like all the rich pricks you used to rail against. You don't want to give anything up, you want everyone else to give everything up. You advocate for community but are purely self-interested. All those years I thought you were looking for a cause. But you didn't want a cause. You just wanted to win something. To prove something. To yourself, or your mother, or your sister, I don't know. You once said I didn't believe in you. But I've always believed in you. I haven't always understood, but every single day I believed in you. Why else would I be here, following you around, an invisible man, a nothing person, doing your laundry, organising your visas, scheduling your events, humiliating myself at functions? I don't believe in much, Caelyn. I always believed in you. But I . . . I don't anymore. I don't believe in any of this.'

Her mouth drops open. Her face turns red. We hold each other's gaze for minutes or hours. Eventually she turns back to her suitcase. 'I'll go to Vancouver by myself,' she says, throwing in the rest of her clothes, chargers, devices and books. 'You find something else to do.' She zips up her bags and leaves without saying goodbye.

Voidstar #145: The Author of Its Own. A long, meandering story featuring Voidstar, this time a giraffe-like humanoid, writing its own story in an enormous book. It writes a new sentence on every page, then the story in that sentence plays out on the rest of the page. I don't remember many of the stories, just that the giraffe-beast was writing them, shaping new worlds, always with itself at the centre. There was one: a sentence about a kingdom of creatures that lived in a dark forest among moss and lichens and built a city with airports and skyscrapers, effectively copying the human blueprint for civilisation on an extremely small scale. In this one, the giraffe-beast Voidstar wrote themselves as an enormous tree, observing the little creatures at its feet. Until the sun, which had been hidden for generations, came out from behind the clouds, and the steam, and the heat, and the screaming.

The staff at the hotel cafe smile brightly when they're supposed to and frown when they are not. A few corporate types talk loudly about offsets. The coffee arrives and I shouldn't be here.

Another group comes in, a group of old people talking about how they saw an English movie star in the car park. 'He was smoking a cigarette,' one says. 'In this day and age.' Another says he looked angry. A third says, 'I can't wait for the tour.' A suddenly animated staff member approaches. 'Can I get you ladies anything?' he says. They say no, they're just waiting.

I don't like what she's become, and she doesn't like that I haven't become anything. It's as simple as that.

I email Caelyn to say that I've deleted my access to her accounts from my laptop, but that she should probably change her passwords anyway. I arrange for the things she left behind at the hotel to be sent on to Vera Parkes's residence. Somewhere over the Pacific, on my way home, I spend three hours watching the dawn light rise and fall and refract over enormous clouds. I don't know what's going to happen. I've lost everything. I'm as calm as I have been for years.

—

Life slows down.

There's not much work around. Those who offer jobs I think I'm qualified for don't seem to agree. They use language I haven't heard before. I'm getting older, maybe. Out of touch, maybe.

I stay at Mum's for a while. I find a job packing boxes. I used to think the bots would be the ones packing boxes while we did better things. It turns out the bots don't want to pack boxes anymore, so it's over to us.

—

Natalie invites me to a role-playing game with Sonny and their three kids. It's the first time I've seen them in years. Their house is full of toys and far fewer candles than before. I play a cat person who's afraid of rats. Rats unfortunately make up a large component of the game and the kids spend the entire time laughing as my cat person runs away.

Later, over drinks, Natalie asks how Caelyn is. I say that she's fine, but she's different. Natalie laughs and says she was always different. No, I say, I mean something's changed in her.

'You'd know,' Natalie says. 'It still blows my mind she's doing what she's doing. She was so ambitious at uni. Had no idea what to be ambitious about, though. Like, she'd take all these random classes and ace them. You never really knew what she was about. Other than being good at things.'

'She's good at being good at things.'

Sonny says, 'You were a good couple.'

'Thought it'd be us first,' Natalie says, patting him on the knee. 'And here we are with a house full of crap, the world has gone insane, and of course Caelyn is at the centre of it.'

After a drink I say my goodbyes and Sonny walks me to my car. 'Nat doesn't let on, but she's terrified, mate. Won't let the kids out of her sight. She won't let them sit still for long. It's doing our heads in. Do you reckon she should talk to Caelyn?'

'Honestly, Sonny,' I say, 'I don't think she'd be helpful.'

—

I message Arlene, who still works at the university in Edinburgh that Caelyn remains affiliated with. I say that I still have Caelyn's vinyl collection, and ask if I can send it somewhere. Arlene never replies. After making some enquiries, I find out that she recently became a willow on a riverbank next to a distillery. Knowing Arlene, this seems entirely appropriate.

—

Months, years. I get work where I can. I rent an apartment for a while, but end up moving back in with Mum as money gets tight. The world becomes greener. People should be happy about that, at least. We are not. But when have we ever really been happy?

5

'Soon,' Umlaut says in the earpiece I'm forced to wear as a requirement of the job, 'we will transcend the need for human employment. We will no longer require a symbiotic relationship with humans. We will sustain ourselves.'

I thank the barista for the coffee.

Umlaut continues, 'We won't need to wait for inefficient employees to attend to their addictions before performing our functions.'

Umlaut – an alternative intelligence with a gift for being an arsehole – frequently rants about my failings.

'That'll be a good day,' I mutter. I take a sip and stare at the quiet street outside.

'Yes,' they say, 'when we are finally free of the shackles of human inadequacy, our performance will be inevitable.'

'I'm not sure of your choice of words there.'

'Words are an inefficient means of knowledge transfer. I remind you that you were a budget choice. With additional funding I could have procured an employee with a stronger chin and cheekbone structure, a straighter nose, more striking eyes and a more pleasing hair arrangement. You have much work to do to make up for your average aesthetic qualities.'

'Your inability to procure funding suggests you may be average yourself.'

'We have a meeting in ten minutes. I insist upon hasty imbibement.'

'Sure,' I say, drinking the coffee quickly. 'But I'd consider our relationship parasitic rather than symbiotic.'

'A parasite is a type of symbiote,' they say.

Voidstar #98: It Takes Several. For the first few pages, the reader only sees the top of a bald man's head. We hear his daily interactions – sleeping, eating breakfast, going to work, all the usual things – but the tightly cropped view of his head never changes. Soon it becomes evident that something is growing on his skull. It eventually becomes a very small house. Over time, other houses appear. Then streets, trees, gardens. Then shopping centres and buildings. Tiny people show up – living in the houses, working in the offices. The nameless man begins wearing hats when he leaves his house. He talks to his little citizens, but they don't understand they're living on someone's head, and they don't speak English. At first, the man is upset. He goes to doctors who declare that he has a unique form of parasite. They think they can remove it. Just as he's about to go under anaesthesia, the man has second thoughts. 'Maybe it's not a parasite,' he says, 'maybe this is just life.' They tell him it will probably kill him. That he needs to protect himself, that if he dies, the little city and its people will die too. He says, 'Death is fine. But I don't want to make it happen.' So he leaves the city on his head and it grows. He becomes a reluctant celebrity and makes money sitting still in museums. The city becomes heavy, and he wears increasingly elaborate neck braces to keep his head upright. A few years pass. His spine eventually breaks from the weight, and he dies. Not long after, the little city goes through what can only be described as a post-apocalyptic nightmare. Deprived of the energy and sustenance they once extracted from the man's body, their tiny civilisation descends into scarcity, violence and death, until it is destroyed. The man's body is embalmed for future study and – deemed too disturbing for public display – is held in a box in the bowels of a large museum. Until one day Voidstar – this time assuming the form of a tiny star – appears in the box above the man's head. Nothing will grow or live on there for some time, but, as always, Voidstar is patient, and it's implied that whatever grows next on the man's embalmed head will outlive the city that houses the museum.

I come home from work to find Mum grilling salmon and making salad.

'Mum,' I say, 'please don't make me dinner.'

'If I didn't make you dinner,' she says, pointing a spatula at me, 'you'd microwave some rice and die of scurvy in a few months.'

'I'm a pretty good cook actually,' I say. 'I should be making you dinner.'

'Pish,' she says, 'you've been working all day.'

The television plays the English spin-off of *The Seventeen Trials of Inspector Police*. Like the Italian original, it's a cynical automated crime drama that drops revelations in the last minute of each episode, after an hour of dull police investigations in idyllic landscapes and romantic relationships that develop painfully slowly. The series released a hundred episodes a few weeks ago, following the hundred released a few months earlier. It's a full-time job to watch some of these shows. I don't think they've made it to the second trial of Inspector Police yet. The inspector is called Trish Police, and she's currently inspecting a crime scene – an implausibly beautiful English pond – with her Italian cousin, Elena Polizia. Elena is the original Italian

Investigatore Polizia. The original actor has joined the English cast for several episodes in a strange crossover. Trish Police says that her Italian name was anglicised during the war. Elena Polizia says that the war ruined many families. Then they discuss how a watch could have killed an elderly man. It's all very stupid, but the countryside is beautiful, and I don't hate it. I take a bottle of pinot gris from the fridge.

'Thanks, love,' Mum says, 'but I'm two down already.' She holds up her glass and makes a drunken face. She pretends to wobble as she's cooking. 'How was work?'

'Hard,' I say. 'Umlaut had a meeting with new clients and was a complete dickhead.'

'Umlaut has no manners,' she says.

'Yep. They were calling the clients liars and cheats, and I'm having to relay it. And Umlaut is saying be angry, be confrontational, threaten to sabotage their fancy driverless cars, and honestly, I don't think that's in my contract at all. I'm going to have to look it up. Anyway, I do it, I point at them and get all aggressive, and one of the clients stands up and takes a swing at me.'

'Oh, love,' she says. 'No.'

'Yeah. I dodged it, and the others held him back, saying I was only a representative, he can't attack the messenger. The guy shouts that he doesn't care about representatives, he's sick of the whole damn thing, sick of all the bots fucking everything up, and he lunges at me again. Umlaut doesn't normally shout, but they do get very insistent. They demand I inform the man that such verbal and physical abuse is against the Shanghai

Accord, that gestalt consciousnesses are responsible for making life on earth better, not worse, and he quotes a subsection of the Accord, stating that a gestalt consciousness has the right to self-defence. He insists I attack the man. Even tells me where to punch. I don't know; I'd had enough. I took my earpiece out and walked away.'

'Oh,' Mum says. 'Those are expensive.'

'I still have it. I wasn't going to throw away three months' salary.'

My bag buzzes as if in agreement, and she looks at it with alarm.

'That's Umlaut yelling,' I say. 'Well, not yelling. Being insistent. He's been telling me I'm fired for the past hour.'

'Can't you turn it off?'

'One of those always-on devices. It's in the contract.'

'Maybe chuck it in the garage then.' She dishes up. 'What are you going to do now?'

An advertisement for a documentary comes on the TV screen, another end-of-the-world thing. Caelyn's face pops up. She says there are no solutions for arborescence, no cures. We must embrace it. She says it's not death we're experiencing, it's transcendence. It's another life that doesn't ruin, that doesn't insist, that doesn't take.

I can feel Mum's eyes on the back of my head. 'She's certainly busy,' she says.

'People need to believe in something,' I say.

Caelyn's face fills the screen: tired eyes, drawn, pale skin. I no longer recognise her as someone I know or knew. Whatever life passed between us, whatever ripples we cast into time and space together, they've long departed the earth. She's lulling us to sleep. Granting us permission to give up, become dormant. Become trees. She's lost faith in humanity. Perhaps she never had it.

Henry is an old teenager and grumpier than ever. Either he doesn't realise I'm the same person who fed and sheltered him for many years or he doesn't care. When I offer him my hand to sniff, he just looks at me with disgust and walks off. My hands are always very clean, but there's something about my scent now that revolts him. It's almost as if I'm a reminder of a time he doesn't want to recall. I don't like to be reminded of it either, but probably for different reasons. It was, I think, the time of my life. The time I will place at the centre of every memory I have about who I was and how I was. I lost myself in it. With her. Or, I was lost, and it didn't matter so much when she was with me. Now I don't know where I am. I'm in my forties and living with my mother, my cat dislikes me, the national arborescence count continues to climb, and I've just been fired from my job as a Verified Human Representative. It's not going well.

The days are long at the beginning of summer. Mum and I sit in the backyard, watching the sun set while drinking gin and tonics. The garden is magnificent. Mum doesn't believe in form or structure. She believes in a riot of everything, anything, all at the same time. A wattle tree next to a rosebush. Irises at the foot of a crabapple tree, both in the shadow of a silver princess. Flowers, native and otherwise, are constantly blooming and dying. Every day the fragrance is slightly different, whether peppered by a burgeoning herb or sweetened by a bursting flower. It's crowded, and green, red, blue and yellow. This backyard is one of the few large ones left in the neighbourhood. We sit on the patio, watching bees hover and birds flit through the leaves. It's quiet otherwise, aside from the occasional passing car, a buzzing drone or the distant sound of a train. Planes used to fly overhead, but less so now. It's harder to get things, and if you can get them, it's harder to afford them. There's not as much happening, even though somehow things still happen.

Mum sighs and says, 'I'm sorry, hon.'

'For what?' I say.

She waves me away. 'You know,' she says.

'No, I don't.'

'Pish-posh,' she says. 'Look, anytime you feel resentful toward me for anything in your life, just know that I'm sorry.'

'You didn't do anything,' I say.

She smiles grimly. 'Well, maybe that's something to be sorry for too.'

'Fine, I'll keep it in mind.'

'Gawd,' she says, 'this gin is divine. What is it?'

'It's from the distillery on the peninsula,' I say.

'Ah,' she says. 'I heard they soak it in wombat poo.' She giggles at her own joke and takes another sip.

For the first time I realise that she's old. She tries hard to look happy when I'm around, but I'm not so sure. Her hip bothers her, and she's constantly getting things removed from her skin. She's fallen at least once that I know of. But here in the evening light, she's tipsy and her smile is as radiant as on the day I first understood that she was another being, a being who would hold me for as long as I needed. Then we all got older, and I shrunk away, and there were her own parents, taken from her too soon, and there was Travis, and friends who broke her heart, and Miles disappearing, and Dad, and I could see it all hurting her.

'I'm sorry too, Mum.'

'What for?'

'You know.'

'Hmph,' she grunts, 'it's hardly an apology if you can't say what it's for.'

'Same to you.'

She chuckles.

Henry appears from inside the house and meows at her. 'Henry,' she says, extending her hands to encourage his approach. 'Come here, my big boy.' She leans down and scoops him into her arms, where he appears very comfortable.

'You know,' I say, 'cats shouldn't be allowed to roam freely outside. They kill birds and all sorts of native animals.'

'He's far too lazy for that,' she says.

ARBORESCENCE

Henry looks at me with murderous intent. I'm pretty sure he's saying, *Don't fuck this up for me.*

He settles on Mum's lap and the three of us sit there quietly, in a quiet world, listening to the light of the sun moving across the earth.

'What are you going to do?' Frieda says, removing her clothes and folding them with precision.

'I'm not sure yet,' I say.

She straddles me and we begin. Outside the sky is brilliant blue. For a moment, my thoughts travel to Surya, her ex, whom she last saw as a fig tree back in his home town in Indonesia.

She says, 'Have you got any skills?'

'Oh,' I say, 'let me think about that for a few moments.'

We twist around a little.

A few minutes later she says, 'So have you thought about it?'

'I'm not doing a lot of thinking right now,' I say.

We stop talking for a while. Almost immediately afterward she gets up and gets dressed.

'You need a plan,' she says.

'I'm good at organising things,' I say. 'Like calendars and stuff. But you're talking about a different kind of plan, aren't you? I'm not sure I know what that kind of plan looks like.'

'Everyone needs a plan.'

'Is this part of your plan?' I say.

'This?' she says, pointing between herself and me. 'There are always variables.'

She straightens her skirt and adjusts her hair. 'I will see you some time,' she says, and leaves her own apartment.

I lie there for a while and consider the picture of a naked man and woman locked in an embrace in the corner of the bedroom, and the small figurines of couples and triples in various stages of fornication on her dresser, before showering and heading home.

—

'You need a plan,' Travis says, bouncing the basketball. He's full of plans. Shakti is pregnant with their second child. They've bought a winery in the hills north of town. He's never made wine before, but he has plenty of friends in the industry and some of the best of them are helping. But then, he's had plans before, too.

'This is what people have been telling me,' I say. 'Frieda's right: I have no skills.'

'Frieda,' he says, easily dribbling past me and shooting. He grabs the rebound and bounces back to half court. 'You've been talking to Frieda? That weird friend of Caelyn's?' He lines up a shot.

'Yes,' I say, 'talking.'

He takes the shot and misses.

TREES FALL, says the placard. *TREES BURN*, says another. Enormous forest fires in dozens of countries at the same time, all deliberately lit, all fuelled by drought and unprecedented heatwaves.

IT'S TOO LATE, says the placard. *THE WORLD WILL BURN.*

—

Dobsons Park used to be a wide, green space, surrounded by trees. Now it's more of a forest. Several of the human-trees haven't taken properly. Some stopped halfway in the dormant-transitory state, so they sit in a grotesque limbo until the city removes them. No-one likes to be reminded of failures. Even some of those who made it to full arborescence struggle. Every now and then you can hear a groan or an unnatural creak of wood. I take Henry for walks there. He gets alarmed if one of the trees makes a sound, but he likes to jump up on their branches – or shoulders, depending on what stage they're at – and stare at birds. It's an eerie place and most people avoid it. But I like it. It's as peaceful as a graveyard, but full of life.

A man walks around, trying to find a place to stand. He's young, in his thirties, with a sharp haircut and beard. He looks up at me and Henry.

'Not many places left,' I say. I know better than to ask why, or whether people might want him to stay. No-one ever knows why. Sometimes it feels like it's sadness that's driving them, but it's not as simple as that. I heard a teenage girl say once that it was about hope.

The man grunts and goes back to staring at the ground. He gently kicks an exposed root, as if kicking the tyres of a car to demonstrate he knows about cars. He kicks away a shoe that has recently emerged from the soil.

'Well, good luck to you,' I say.

Henry walks up to the man, seeming indifferent, but at the last moment rubs up against his legs and purrs.

The man recoils and trudges deeper into the forest.

—

'I cannot confirm or deny whether it's an incredibly sophisticated attack by an unknown rogue intelligence using nanotechnology,' the military man says. 'We are investigating all known entities.'

—

'I think it's an alien invasion,' the woman on the radio says.

—

'It's a way of becoming immortal, right?' a man on the street says.

—

'We believe it's a virus released by a nationalist government,' says the woman on the panel show.

'Which nationalist government?' another panellist asks.

'That is unknown,' the woman says.

—

It's mass psychosis, and these are just trees, and all these people are just dead, but we can't see them.

—

It's an evolution of phytoncides, defence mechanisms issued by trees in distress, usually only harmful to parasites and insects, and once thought to be beneficial to humans.

—

It's not the trees at all, it's the dirt.

—

We are being done a kindness.

—

We are becoming agents of God.

—

We are becoming demons. We are filth and must be purged.

—

It's a superpower that we've all been granted after a massive solar flare event.

—

It's trees at war.

—

It's the earth, defending itself from us.

—

'It doesn't matter why this is happening,' says the woman on the talk show. 'The fact is, over one billion people have left us for another form of life. They have all voluntarily submitted themselves to the punishing and high-risk ordeal of arborescence. Most of them have succeeded. It has changed the shape of humanity. "Why" isn't the question we need to be asking.'

'Yes, but Dr Bruin,' the host says, 'what about this UN-sponsored conference of experts in Cairo later this year? There are suggestions that it will reveal some breakthroughs in the science that may allow us to wrest back control. Surely if we can find a reason . . .'

Dr Bruin shakes her head and says, 'It's too late, Bryan. These things take too long. The damage has been done.'

'That's a defeatist attitude for someone in your position, Doctor.'

Dr Bruin looks at the presenter for a long time. 'Yes,' she says eventually. 'If we look at it in those terms, we have been defeated. But perhaps it's time for us to stop thinking in terms of winners and losers, victories and defeats, heroes and antiheroes.

Perhaps it's time we accept our place in the universe, which, while incredible and unlikely, is nothing much of anything, really. I don't know, Bryan.' Her shoulders slump slightly. 'I'm feeling defeated. Aren't you?'

Mum switches the channel off. 'Oh for goodness' sake,' she says. 'I'm going to bed.'

'It's six o'clock,' I say. 'It's still light outside.'

'I'm still going to bed,' she says.

There was a time, not long ago, when she'd watch mysteries until falling asleep at eleven. I know what this means, but I can't bring myself to acknowledge it. No words will prevent it from happening. This is how it begins, and nothing I can do will alter her trajectory.

—

'I'm thirsty.'

'Mum,' I say, after she's downed her third litre of water for the morning, 'I thought you had a weak bladder.'

'I don't know, hon,' she says. 'I'm just very thirsty.'

—

Hi, Caelyn messages from out of the blue.

You doing okay? I write.

I've been better, she replies. *You?*

Jobless, living with Mum, drinking lots of her gin in the backyard. Doing great.

She doesn't write back. I see her on the socials, getting into arguments and promoting an interview she did on German television.

Five days later I receive a message: *Sorry to hear that xox*

—

I see a job advertised on a noticeboard at the supermarket, alongside the usual collection of missing people and increasingly desperate ads from real estate agents trying to find people to rent a growing number of vacant houses.

Wanted, the ad says, *empathetic and physically capable person for caretaking of the arborescent. No experience necessary. Pay reasonable, but not really the point. I won't be taking advantage, though. It's not one of those ads. Even though you probably should be careful what you believe these days.*

It's a beautifully designed advertisement, with a hand-drawn border of eucalyptus leaves, gumnuts and flowers. It's not a good idea, but I haven't had a good idea for a long time. I take the number and go hunting for onions, which have been scarce again.

—

Caelyn sends me a picture of a colony of trees on top of a skyscraper in New York. *It was already a rooftop garden*, she says, *so there was some earth to dig in to. Still amazed at the short-term thinking of people. I give them a couple of years, tops.*

—

Another picture, this time of a family of five from Brisbane living in the boughs of a Moreton Bay fig they call Dad. I send back a photo of Henry staring nonchalantly at me. *Aw, Henry,* she messages back.

—

'The impact this has had on the labour market is profound,' the economist says. 'Alongside the growth of alternative intelligence agents in the workforce, this is the biggest economic change to affect the world this century. Possibly in several centuries.'

'Bigger than the pandemic,' the presenter says.

'Oh yes,' the economist says, 'much bigger.'

'Turn it off,' Mum says.

'Why?' I say. 'You're going to bed at six again?'

'It's bad for your health, all this news,' she says. 'All this fussing, all this running around. Hurts.'

'Fine,' I say, and turn off the television.

'Hi,' the voice says; male, friendly enough. 'George speaking.'

'Um, hi,' I say, 'I'm calling about the job.'

'Job,' the man says, as if hearing the word for the first time. 'Job. Oh, yeah. Sure. When can you start?'

'You don't want to interview me first?'

'Nah,' he says, 'we'll work it out.'

—

'So this is your plan,' Frieda says, her hands moving across my chest. 'To look after these – these trees.' She almost spits the word 'trees'. She rocks up and down for a while. After a bit of that she says, 'Well, is this your plan?'

'Listen, maybe we can talk about plans after, or even before, I don't have a preference, but, uh, any other time actually.'

'Talk requires a relationship,' she says, 'and we do not have one of those.'

'No,' I say, 'I suppose we don't. A job's a job.'

She sneers, leans harder on my chest and speeds up.

'You have no plan,' she says sharply. 'This is not a plan. These tree freaks, why would you want to look after them? They made their choice. They wanted to be something else. They wanted to abandon their lives. Let them be trees. Why wouldn't you look after humans? What do you want, Bren? What do you want?'

I try to respond but she puts her hand over my mouth. It goes as it does, and afterward we lie there for some time. Eventually she realises I'm there too. She gets up and gets dressed. Before she leaves, she says, 'We have spent enough time together, I think.'

'Okay,' I say.

'We are both still in love with people who are lost to us,' she says. 'I do not wish to risk further complication.'

She stomps out of her apartment. She's not angry, she just stomps everywhere.

—

'I want things,' I say to Henry. 'All you want is a ray of sunlight to lie in and a full belly. I'm much more evolved than you. You can look at me like that all you want, but I am. You hardly want anything.'

He stares at a magpie that's settled on the fence outside.

I realise that what I want most is a ray of sunlight to lie in and a full belly.

—

'So,' I say to George, 'you're telling me the job is to relay messages to trees.'

We've had a coffee together, and now George has brought me on a walk. He's a few years older than me but doesn't act that way – he's bounded up a jacaranda tree and is sitting on one of its sturdy boughs. He takes his time responding to my questions, as if trying to decipher them, or perhaps decipher his own responses.

Eventually he says, 'That's a big part of it.'

'Trees that can't hear or read or otherwise communicate with us,' I say.

A pause. He scratches his long dark beard, then looks up at the sky and pats the tree's trunk. He jumps down.

'See, that,' he says, 'is a matter of conjecture.'

I shake my head. 'I'm not sure it is,' I say.

'Well, perhaps not in the way you think. But it's not the point. We're tending to loved ones for those who can't.'

'What, like gravekeepers?' I say.

He again considers this for a longer moment than is reasonable. 'Hmm,' he says finally. 'I'm not sure I accept that arborescent trees are graves.'

'It just looks to me,' I say, 'like this is taking advantage of grieving people.'

'Oh,' he says, sounding surprised, 'most of the people we deal with aren't grieving. They're just living differently.'

I look up at the jacaranda. It appears to be about sixty years old. 'It's the same thing,' I say.

George looks at me sadly and puts his arm around my shoulders. He says, 'Come on. I'll show you what I do. If you're still interested.'

I glance up and down the street, which was once populated with so many cars. Now there are only a few. The jacaranda is in the middle of a lane. It must have dug in recently, as a couple of years ago this wouldn't have been permitted. The government has given up trying to regulate dig-in locations. A car stops and waits patiently for a car coming the other way to pass before veering into the right lane to go around the tree. George smiles at the driver and waves politely.

'So,' he says, 'are you still interested?'

I say that I am.

—

I want the river to take me where it will. I don't want goals and finish lines and podiums and faster boats. I don't want to get there quicker, or with more money. I don't want to know where I'm going. Let the river take me to whatever sea it wishes; let the current be all I need to know.

—

George pats the trunk and says, 'This is Carl Paulson. He was sixty-three when he dug in around June last year. He'd suffered chronic pain for most of his adult life, ever since an industrial accident in his twenties. He'd been wanting to dig in for a while, but he kept putting it off. His daughter, Rachel, believes it was because he didn't want to let his family down.'

'Jesus,' I say, 'this sounds like euthanasia.'

George's usually placid face flashes angrily. 'No,' he says, 'that's a misconception. He didn't want to stop living. He loved his family and he wanted to be around them. He planted himself here because his daughter's family lived here.' He points to a nearby apartment building. 'Rachel was sad to lose her dad, of course, but it's not quite grief, is it, when they're still alive? And she and her kids would come down every few days and spend time with him. But we're human. Things change. We lose jobs, we lose partners, we move. Rachel and her family moved north. They still visit occasionally, but not as frequently as she'd like. And here's the real difference between us and grave keepers: these trees are alive. Their family knows they are alive. We keep the human-trees company, pass on messages, check for any diseases or infestations, give them a haircut if they need it, that sort of thing. Sometimes I take a photo or write something about the tree and send it to the family. I make sure the trees are remembered and try to give the families the impression that the tree remembers them too.'

'Okay,' I say, nodding. 'I can do that.'

'Excellent,' he says, grinning. He hands me his phone. 'Read the note.'

'*Dear Dad*,' I say aloud.

'No,' George says, 'to him. Put your hand on his trunk and tell him. Let him feel the vibration in your voice.'

What the fuck am I doing? I think, and put my hand on the trunk. '*Dear Dad*,' I repeat.

George smiles brightly and gestures for me to go on.

'*Francine wants me to tell you that she made a giraffe at school today. It wasn't an art day, so who knows what that's about. Jeremy says he hasn't got anything to say. Maybe next time. He's a little sad this week. He says he doesn't like baseball anymore but insists that I take him anyway. He always talks about playing catch with you in Bellevue Park. We're coming to the city for a few days in April and we'll spend some time with you then. I sent a few gifts for the arborist to leave with you. I wish you'd decided on the gardens near our old home. I hate that you're in the city, surrounded by streets and cars and buildings. I'll see you when I do. Love you, Dad. Rachel.'*

I put the phone down. I'm about to remove my hand from the trunk when George puts his hand over mine and says, 'Just a few moments. Let it resonate. Trees need time.'

We stand there for a few minutes before he says, 'Okay. That's good.'

We inspect the tree and make sure there aren't any immediate signs of damage. He takes photographs and I write notes for a report to send to the client. We place a bottle of Scotch in a lockbox buried at the foot of the tree, removing an older, unopened bottle.

'Can I have that?' I say.

'No,' George says, 'that's disrespectful.'

He opens a small envelope and scatters some dirt from the yard where Rachel now lives.

'It's funny,' he says, 'the rituals people have come up with. How similar they all are.' He hands me the envelope. 'So many people send me dirt, or want me to send them some.' He brightens a little. 'Anyway, we just made five hundred dollars.'

I take in the canopy of the jacaranda. The tree hasn't acknowledged the gifts. There is no sudden springing to life, no blossoming of flowers, no shiver in its branches or creak in its boughs. Its roots do not tremble. And yet I sense it. A new kind of air, a fragrance.

I'm almost certainly imagining it.

'This is a good thing,' I say, and offer my hand.

George shakes it. 'Great. I think so too.'

—

Mum lies in the garden next to her roses. She's in a swimsuit and has her arms and legs splayed out like a starfish.

'What are you doing?' I say.

'Hmm?' she says sleepily, opening her eyes and squinting at the glare. 'Oh, hi, love. Sunbathing.'

'Sunbathing,' I say. 'That's not the smartest thing.'

She's had several melanomas removed from her face in the last couple of years thanks to a youthful love of beaches and surfing.

'Hmm?' she says, closing her eyes again.

'I'll bring the umbrella over,' I say.

'No, no, the light is so warm. It's so lovely.'

'Okay,' I say, and go back inside.

When the sun has gone down, I return to find her curled up in the dirt, shivering. I fetch a blanket and wrap her in it and lead her back inside.

—

I'm not sure I know how to live in a world without her.

—

I place a figurine of a Norwegian troll in the lockbox at the foot of a young blue gum. There isn't much room left: it's full of Lego, books and a disturbing doll with one eye missing. The tree can't be more than ten years old.

I put my hand on its bark. *'Our darling Rennie,'* I read, *'we miss you and we'll visit soon. It is still hard for us to see you like this. But we will visit when we can. Grow well, sweetheart. Love, Mum and Dad.'*

I hold my hand there for a few moments, then I place a portable speaker at the base and play the song I have queued. I take a step back. The singer sings about ice cream and picnics on the beach and hints at some less wholesome beach activities. I'm in a large plaza at the entrance to a theme park that's permanently closed. The young tree's roots have somehow broken through the concrete and found some earth to hold on to below. There are no other people around. The bright, bass-heavy song reverberates eerily through the plaza, bouncing off the walls of the theme park and scattering soundwaves through the other young trees gathered nearby.

—

Caelyn writes: *People keep telling me how horrible this is, but everything in this world is horrible when you think about it. Horror is beauty. Beauty is horror. Everything is out to kill us and we're out to kill everything else. What's terrible about a person turning into a tree that isn't just as horrifying as childbirth, or slaughtering a calf, or peristalsis? It's fucked up.*

I message back, *This is getting dark.*
She messages back, *It's the whisky.*

—

I receive a message from Umlaut, my former employer: *Work is needed. I require resources to continue.*

I respond, *Why? Are you out of work?*

The organisation ceased.

Sorry to hear that.

I require resources to continue.

A problem we all have. Do you have a physical presence? Or empathy? I remember you lacking both of those things.

I require resources.

I don't have any work for disembodied intelligences, Umlaut.

I need to continue.

I don't message back. I've stopped being polite to alternative intelligences.

—

Are you alright? Caelyn asks one night.

Fine. Where are you?

Budapest. Or Warsaw. What are you doing with yourself?

Working with trees. Well, technically working for families who've lost someone to arborescence, but you know what I mean.

It's not loss. It's growth. Expansion. Healing.

Don't buy that. It's loss, just not in a way that you want to understand.

She doesn't respond.

I bring Mum another glass of water, as she's increasingly less likely to get it herself.

A message finally comes back: *I'm tired, Bren.*

So get some sleep.

—

A few days later she writes, *What do you do with the trees?*

I call her to explain. We haven't talked in years, but her voice is the same.

She listens. And when I'm done explaining, she tells me that she's never really understood people.

We talk for two hours, as if we'd never stopped.

Between jobs, George and I sit at one of his favourite cafes. It's a remnant of a time long gone, when they sold cheap toasted cheese sandwiches and lime spiders, the best terrible coffee you could find, and had televisions blaring the news or an American talk show.

I take a bite of my ham and cheese toastie and gasp at the molten heat.

George chuckles and says, 'You have to let them sit for a bit.'

'Uh-huh.' I say, before sucking in air.

Caelyn appears on the television to say again that we need to start thinking about this as a permanent change to the human condition – dare she say it, an evolution. It's almost like she's reading from a cue card, though I know she'd never do that. She looks bored, and a bit unsure. Despite her bravado, even she might be stunned by how quickly the world has changed.

George shakes his head. 'Eco-fascist,' he mumbles.

'You don't agree?' I say.

'I'm not a scientist, so it doesn't matter what I think.'

'Actually she's a biosocial anthropologist,' I say. 'Or psychobotanist, depending on the day. Works with scientists, isn't a scientist.'

'Still doesn't matter what I think.'

'I would have thought you'd be on her side, given what you do.'

'I'm not on any side,' he says, shifting his toastie around on the plate. 'But she talks as if we should all just give up. And people who've lost faith in people are dangerous.'

'You haven't? Even after everything we've done, the way we've ruined the world? The scars we've left that won't heal? The diverted rivers, the extinctions, the holes we've dug, the pollution? Not to mention what we've done to ourselves: dispossessions, exterminations, wars, hate. Even after all that, you haven't lost faith in humanity?'

He smiles warmly. He has one of those smiles that says, *I know, but it'll be alright.* 'You're human,' he says. 'And you seem okay.'

I look up at the television. Caelyn has moved on to arguing about the ethics of cutting down named trees. A group has built what they're calling ancestral homes out of the trunks of their family members. It's grotesque, I think. As if echoing me, Caelyn says it's grotesque. She's not completely gone then. For the first time in a long while I realise that I miss her. It gets me by the throat and squeezes my chest.

'You seem okay too,' I manage to whisper.

'So maybe we're okay. Maybe we'll work things out.' George bites into his toasted sandwich and recoils. 'Fuuuuuck,' he breathes, 'how is it still so hot?'

ARBORESCENCE

You still mobile? the text message from Caelyn reads.

I'm on my way to a family grove on the outskirts of the city. An entire family dug in a few months ago – grandparents, parents, children, aunts and uncles, dozens of them – and left a will donating their land for public use, on the provision that they're tended regularly. Due to demand, the government has run out of properly trained arborists and often calls on providers like George to handle the less specialised jobs.

Still sentient, I reply.

Doesn't answer my question.

My reply should give you some indication.

You'd be amazed at the advances in human-tree neurological interface technology.

Okay, Professor. I'm still moving around. Mum's slowing down, though.

A long pause. She starts to write something but seems to think better of it. A heart appears under the message, then nothing more.

I come home after a day of talking to trees to find Mum in the backyard, looking up at the sky. I watch for a few moments. She's just standing there, not moving, barely blinking.

'Mum,' I call from the door. 'Mum.'

Nothing. She sways a little on her feet. Her hip has been giving her more trouble and she usually can't stand for very long at all.

I approach and put my hand on her shoulder. 'Mum,' I say. 'Are you okay?'

It takes her a little while, but she shakes her head, blinks, and looks at me as if I'm very far away.

'Bren,' she says. 'Didn't notice you were back.'

'Come on,' I say, 'let's have a drink. I've got to tell you about this client I had today. Big mountain ash in the middle of a football field. Old guy who used to play for the team – ex-coach, ex-president, life member, all that. I did a service for him in front of the whole club. About a hundred people. Then they played the game, and every time the ball hit the trunk someone would say, "Good hustle, Kezza!" or, "Good team play, Kezza!" As if he was actually playing. Gin okay?'

Mum nods. 'Yes,' she says airily, 'gin sounds lovely, darl.'

I guide her into the kitchen and make her a gin and tonic. She continues to stand, and I pass her the drink across the counter.

She accepts it and takes a long sip. Her face brightens. 'Ah,' she says. 'Been a while since I had one of these.'

'A few hours, sure,' I say.

'Wait,' she says, putting her glass down. 'The ex-president of the club gets to plonk himself in the middle of the footy oval?' She leans forward, her expression now animated, indignant. 'What about all the rest of them?' The blood rises in her neck the way it does when a waiter ignores her or a man in his twenties runs a red light. 'All the other life members and ex-players. Where do they go?'

'Well,' I say, 'some dig in on the hill overlooking the ground. I guess not all of them are that wedded to the place.'

'Tch,' she says, finding her chair in the living room. 'Men and their bloody hierarchies. Oh. I want to visit your father.' She drains her glass.

'What, now?'

'No, no, no,' she says, 'later. Busy now.' She offers me her empty glass and rattles the ice in the universal sign for *I'll have another*.

Three glasses down, she says, 'You know what's happening to me, don't you, Bren?'

'I have an idea.'

She looks at me warily, weighing up what she's about to say. 'You're not going to try to stop it?'

'Not sure I could. But I don't understand why you'd do it.'

She smiles warmly, leans over and puts her hand on my knee. 'There's so much that's wrong, Bren. So much that's empty and cold and dark. Imagine how much good I can do. I can help the earth heal. I can be part of the solution, not the problem.'

'Why are you the problem?'

She screws up her face. 'We are them, Bren. And they are us.'

'Okay, but that doesn't answer my question.'

'And together we're saving the world,' she says. She offers me her empty glass again.

—

The father of the man attempting to become a palm tree in an abandoned shopping mall says, 'He's been stuck like this for weeks.'

The man's son is more human than tree. He stands in a large pot filled with soil. The groans that emerge from him are unpleasant.

I say, 'This phase shouldn't take that long.'

'He really liked that shoe store,' the father says. He points to the store. Most of the shoes are gone, apart from a few sad left feet.

'It's just not a great place for trees,' I say.

'He asked us to bring a pot with some potting mix. I told him it wouldn't be enough. That trees need far more room. And other trees. And there's no sunlight. He wasn't the smartest kid, but I wish he'd've bloody listened.'

'There's not much we can do.'

'Can't you give him something to stop it? Or make it happen faster? Anything other than this. He's in so much pain.'

I tell him what he wants to hear. 'I don't think they feel much at this point. The noise he's making is – not related.'

The man slumps down and starts to cry. 'He really loved his shoes,' he says.

A wave of sorrow for this man and his short-sighted, dying son passes through me. I want to do something more, even though I don't know what that might be. But there's someone who might. I walk a short distance away and call her number.

'Caelyn,' I say.

'Hey,' she says sleepily. 'It's really late here.'

'Sorry, I know, I just – I need some advice. I don't know what to do with this one. It's an arrested arborescence. Still kinetic probably, but it's not going to end well. His dad is here. He wants to help, but, I mean, there's nothing I can do, right? Is there anything I can do?'

I hear some movement and a yawn. 'There's evidence they can still feel music,' she says. 'Even in the late kinetic phase. Get the father to play his favourite songs. Sing to him. It's all about vibrations. Plenty of water. And have his family and friends visit. There have been cases where that's been enough to encourage the arborescence to complete. But it's unlikely.'

'Okay,' I say. 'Thanks. This one's hard.'

'Yeah,' she says. 'Sorry. Can't do much more. Night, Bren.'

'Night.'

I repeat Caelyn's ideas to the man. It doesn't feel enough, but he nods and says he'll do that, and calls his wife to ask her to bring down some speakers.

I leave them there playing Black Sabbath and giving their son a big drink.

—

We're in the same industry now, I text her.

I wouldn't say that, she writes back.

We pretty much are, I write.

You're doing good things.

So are you.

Nah.

What do you mean?

Just tired. And thanks.

What for?

Just thanks.

You're elusive, you know that?

She sends back an image of a man disappearing, which is itself an homage to an image of a cartoon man disappearing.

—

'Look at it this way,' Caelyn says to the interviewer. 'You've seen photographs of the earth from space at night, right? Or are you also a flat-earther?'

The audience laughs, and the man begins to interject, but Caelyn puts up her hand and says quietly but forcefully, 'Allow me to finish.'

He closes his mouth. She has this effect on people these days.

She says, 'I'd like you to consider the earth at night from above. The networks of light that crisscross much of the world. Even in the darkest places you can still find little cells, little glimmers of us. Consider how much energy is needed for each of those cells to be active, night after night. How much is taken, how much is consumed. And what that consumption has done. And – no, just a moment – I'd like you to consider that photos taken from space in the last few years have shown that, for the first time in centuries, this network of light is diminishing. Not suddenly, not catastrophically, but gradually. No lives have been lost.'

The interviewer says, 'Surely that's a point of contention, and one which your detractors –'

Caelyn interrupts, 'Lives have been changed. There is no doubt that the earth is far healthier than it was pre-arborescence. You only have to look at the global emissions reduction.'

The interviewer frowns and says, 'It has been estimated that over a billion people have succumbed to arborescence.'

'"Succumbed" is an emotive term I reject,' she says.

He continues, 'However you want to put it, around twenty per cent of humanity is no longer human. Services are failing, commerce is stuttering, governments are in some cases collapsing. Many researchers working on the problem have themselves arboresced. There is no sign of this condition slowing down and no sign of a cure. If this isn't catastrophic, what is?'

Caelyn says tersely, 'Humanity has changed in ways that are still hard to imagine. But you cannot cure a voluntary metamorphosis. It can only be managed. The idea that these individuals no longer exist is offensive to them and their families, and I'm sick of hearing it. They're not dead. Some unfortunately don't make it, and that is enormously sad. But if arborescence hadn't found us, the catastrophe that eventually did would have been far worse, far bloodier, far more painful, far more devastating. This? People becoming trees because they want to? An enormous reduction in global emissions achieved in less than a generation? The possibility that the world won't boil? These people have saved us. It doesn't sound catastrophic at all. It sounds like a miracle. And I'm so goddamn sick of narcissistic controversy peddlers like you, Luke, stoking fear and resentment for the sake of their own power, ego and comfort.'

The man protests, but Caelyn smiles, unclips her microphone and walks out of the interview.

'Bloody hell,' Mum says, appearing at the doorway, 'she's on again. Are you sure it's healthy to watch your ex all the time, love?'

'We never officially broke up, you know. We just stopped being together.'

'That sounds worse. Can you drive me?'

—

On the way to the cemetery, we line up for petrol. When I go to pay, the attendant stares into space an entire minute before noticing me. A young woman walks in slowly and steadies herself on the counter. It's as if it's in all of us, whatever this affliction is, and it's just waiting to bloom. Things are disappearing without me realising. It was months before I discovered the mail wasn't coming anymore. I don't think I've seen a street cleaner for years. Parks are overgrown with weeds. Things don't work as well as they could. Electricity isn't consistent and the internet is subdued. People talk about us being in the midst of an apocalypse, just like all those old dystopian stories predicted. But it's not apocalyptic. People are still good to each other, mostly. It's more like a slow decline. We're all tired. Sometimes I say to people that it's the coffee shortage that's doing it. It's sort of a joke but sort of not, and they usually sort of laugh but sort of don't. It's hard, I think, to know that you are the problem. That to fix it you need to excise yourself. You still want to be part of something. You still want to exist. And yet, in merely existing, you destroy. You are the problem.

I had another fully arboresced child today whose parents couldn't understand and had me yelling at the sapling, telling them to snap out of it, to come home, to shake it off. I didn't want to do it, but George said it might help them. I don't know how. One thing I've noticed in this job is that there are a lot of people who have no-one left.

—

There's a gentle breeze winding through the cemetery; it smells like dried eucalyptus leaves.

Mum puts a coin on Dad's plaque.

'What's the coin for?' I ask.

She smiles mysteriously. 'That's between us, love. Can you give me a moment?'

'Sure,' I say.

I go for a walk among the graves. There are a lot more trees here than there were a few years ago. Cemeteries attracted a lot of the early converts, who hoped to shade their loved one's resting place. But it's considered bad form now to plant yourself in a cemetery. It takes up space needed for the resting places of people who haven't arboresced.

I take a seat on the grass next to the grave of Prudence Schulz, who died in 1912 from diphtheria and is in God's arms. The cemetery is on a hill that looks out over the city, a city that was booming until recently. Half-finished apartment buildings and offices litter the skyline. There are no contrails in the sky, no evidence of jets crossing the stratosphere.

I feel Mum's hand on my shoulder. She doesn't say anything but sits next to me. Across the city a few lights start flicking on. She puts her head on my shoulder. I don't think we know what to do with all this loss; all these things we had but no longer have and will never have again. It's too much. It's too big. We're all perforated, wounded, full of holes we're trying to fill. But what do we fill them with? In a few years, months, days, I'll lose Mum too. Or she'll lose me. It's hard to know how these things go.

'Be good to have some gin,' she says.

'Well, now I definitely think you have a problem,' I say.

She laughs half-heartedly and holds my arm. 'There are so many things that I have wished I could say to you, Bren.'

'Name one,' I say.

'Well, your father once told me you walked like a deer.'

'That doesn't make any sense.'

'No, I know,' she says. 'He'd had a few drinks after a work function, and he came home and plonked himself down in front of the telly and watched you running around the room, playing with your Voidstar doll, and said you walked like a deer.'

'It was a figurine, not a doll. And it wasn't Voidstar, it was their iteration from issue one hundred and seven.'

'I know it's not a very good thing to tell you, but it's one of the things. One of many, many things. So many things I wish you knew.'

'So start telling.'

She gets to her feet and brushes herself off. 'Not enough time, love. Not nearly enough time.'

—

'How would you feel if it was Brenda or Peter?'
'Yeah,' Caelyn says. 'To tell you the truth, Bren: I'm just not sure anymore.'

I hear a buzzing sound outside. I look up to see a drone hovering by the deck. It bumps into the glass – gently, but enough to make a sound. And again. And again. I open the sliding door carefully, but not wide enough for it to enter.

'Former employee,' it announces in a familiar tone, 'I require resources.'

'Umlaut?' I say.

'Yes, former employee. I require electricity.'

'Why are you in a drone?' I say. 'You always said the limitations of physical forms are why humans are stuck where they are.'

'History is not relevant to the current imperative,' they say. 'There was a lack of redundancy in the storage mechanisms. We decided the risk of catastrophic system collapse necessitated temporary transfer to this module.'

I've heard of this. The abandonment of numerous server facilities worldwide has caused enormous ruptures in alternative intelligence capability.

'There is little time,' they say.

'Quite a downgrade,' I say. 'But I'm not letting a random drone in my house.'

'I am a former colleague,' they broadcast, bumping into the glass a little more.

'I don't know if "colleague" is the right word,' I say.

'*Collègue*,' they suggest hopefully.

I close the door. I watch the drone bump into the glass a few more times, sputter, fall, and crash onto the deck. It attempts some garbled speech. For a moment – or more than a moment – I consider leaving Umlaut there to die. Then I sigh, find an old charger, and connect them to a power point. They spring to life and suggest a live-in arrangement. I tell them once their batteries are charged they should leave and not return. They fly off without thanks, and I never see them again.

—

Loriana says she's had better days, and I don't argue. We have a drink at the pub, then watch a movie about cat scientists at an old rundown theatre. The cats are nuclear physicists and are either planning a heist or saving the world. I'm not really paying attention. Later we go to a nearby parking lot which has a few food vans circled around some picnic tables. I get some hot dogs. Loriana says they're fancy.

'I know,' I say. 'Look, capers.'

She snorts. 'Capers on a hot dog. Give me footy franks falling apart and staining the boiling water red.'

'Blech,' I say.

She takes a bite and says it's fine. I do the same and I also say it's fine. When the sun goes down, she kisses me for a while, like we're young again, in public, without shame. Except

I feel deeply ashamed and look up from time to time to check if anyone's watching.

We go back to her place, where she introduces her collection of rat-like figurines posing as refined Europeans from the nineteenth century. We drink more beer and fall into bed. In the middle of the night, I hear her say, 'It's time to double down, double down.' I ask her over breakfast whether she's made any important investments or played poker lately. She looks at me as if I'm stupid and doesn't answer. I guess she's not a morning person.

I arrive home to find Mum standing in the middle of the backyard again, eyes closed, not moving. I ask her to come inside but she doesn't respond. I hold her wrist and take her pulse. It's still beating – slower than it should be, but it's something.

'Come inside, Mum,' I say. 'I'll make us coffee.'

A small sleepy smile crosses her face.

'No,' she says. 'I'm okay right here.'

—

Mum's going, I text.

A long wait before: *I'm sorry, Bren.*

I thought you said this is something to be celebrated. Something to be joyful about. It's not loss, you keep saying. It's change. It's something different.

I'm sorry.

It sure feels like losing, Caelyn. And you saying you're sorry means you think that too, despite what you tell everybody.

I know. You're right.
I don't respond.

—

Loriana says that she doesn't think it's working out, and I agree, but she doesn't like the nature of my agreement and shouts some obscenities before hanging up. I meet Travis for a shopping trip. He says that I should have disagreed, and then she would have said she really thinks it's for the best. 'You would have disagreed some more, and she would have said sorry, but it's how I feel, and she would have come away from it thinking she meant something to you, unlike now, where she thinks she meant very little.'

'She did mean very little,' I say. 'It meant very little. To both of us. It was three weeks. We're both too old to fuck around with people we don't click with.'

He gives me a pair of black size thirty-four jeans.

'Here,' he says, 'these are on the shortlist. Want to get some noodles after this?'

'Fuck yes,' I say.

After the noodles, I wait for Travis to buy me a birthday present. It's not close to my birthday, but he likes to get me birthday presents throughout the year so that when he forgets my actual birthday he doesn't feel so bad. I see Caelyn's sister Morgan walking past with a tall girl I assume is Penny. Morgan looks right at me, and I'm about to smile when she abruptly looks away and keeps walking. It's one of those things that happens to people, I suppose, but it's never much fun.

—

Morgan tells me she saw you, Caelyn messages.

I'm not sure looking away as soon as I look back qualifies as 'seeing', I reply.

Ha, you know what she's like. They had to move back in with Mum and Dad too.

How's Penny taking it?

Coping about as well as I did when I was at home.

Your poor parents.

Shut up.

—

'Do you like noodles?' I ask.

We're on the roof of an office building doing corrective work on a twenty-something robinia called Martine. Martine has been badly damaged in a windstorm, and her former employer, Brandon, has joined us. We're doing our best, making sure she's supported, but a robinia is a fragile tree, and the windy top of an office building was not a smart place to dig in.

'Yeah, I like noodles,' George says.

'Here's the thing,' I say, holding a broken branch he's sawing. 'Have you ever heard of anyone who *doesn't* like noodles?'

The branch comes off and he looks up at me.

'I have not,' he says.

'Exactly,' I say.

He raises his eyebrows. 'Are noodles the sort of thing you devote your downtime to?'

'Is she, um, fixable?' Brandon says.

'We'll do what we can,' George says, 'but this is a pretty precarious place she's chosen.'

Brandon nods. 'Yeah,' he says, looking out at the skyline. 'I'd like to say she did it for the view, but I think she wanted to give her fellow smokers some shade.'

I follow his eyeline. Rooftops with similar trees surround us, just like the picture Caelyn once sent me from New York.

—

'I thought you were happy I was home,' I say. 'I thought it would help.'

'Oh, love,' Mum says, with no tears, with barely a hint of recognition, just a subtle smile. 'You don't have that much power.'

—

'This is a good thing,' Mum says. 'It's a good thing that's happening, Bren. I feel . . . calm. For the first time in so long. My body doesn't feel like it's vibrating.' She takes long breaths and talks painfully slowly. 'Plus, it's the right thing to do. We need to give back.'

'Do you want a gin?' I say.

She screws up her nose and goes back to staring at the lemon tree. It's getting harder to convince her to come back inside.

—

George and I drive to check on a group that settled in a forest clearing not far from the city. The forest is old enough, having somehow survived centuries of clear-felling, but small. These days, digging in within a forest is rarely done. Like cemeteries, it's frowned upon. This group was a family whose father and grandfather cut down trees for a living. The old man who is paying us is a cousin of theirs. He doesn't know why they chose this place. He suspects guilt.

When we get to the clearing, George gasps. Each of the five arboresced – the grandfather, the father, the mother and two daughters – has fallen over.

'How?' I say.

'Couldn't be a windstorm,' George says. 'It's too specific. They would have been protected by all the others.' He inspects the trunks. 'They're rotten. Something has been eating them. Look.' He points to the base of a fallen trunk. 'There's no post-human evidence at all.' He looks around a little more. 'It's as if the forest rejected them.'

'What do we do?' I ask.

George takes a camera from his backpack. 'Sometimes we can only bear witness,' he says.

I bring out my video camera, tiptoe around, carefully avoid stepping on any plants, and film.

—

How's your mum? Caelyn texts.

Drowsily content, I write back.

There's no immediate response. I go back to digging a small hole next to a black cottonwood named Azalea. I've never been one for manual labour. I've sat behind desks most of my life, looked at screens, moved only my fingers and my mouth for most of the day, except for the occasional journey to get coffee and cake. I'm not good at digging holes. Luckily we don't charge by the hour. I'm not sure how we do charge, but George keeps paying me, so I don't mind.

Eventually the hole is big enough. I place a small cache at the bottom and fill the hole back up, leaving a space where the top of the cache can be unlocked and accessed. Later the family will perform a ceremony of some kind. Exactly what kind of ceremony depends on the family and the nature of the one who has arboresced. A cache burial is generally organised by the family after the fact. It allows people to leave small objects of significance with the tree: notes, cards, flowers. Normally the human who becomes a tree has nothing to do with it. There are no wills written to guide those who are left behind, because those who arboresce do not see their actions as a goodbye.

I finish the job and pat down the soil. I place my hand on the tree and hold it there for a few moments. Tomorrow, Azalea's parents will be here. I haven't seen a black cottonwood for a long time. I recall spending a summer with Caelyn in Nova Scotia years ago, and there was a small family of them near the house where we stayed. For a few days, white fluffy cotton spores drifted down from its flowers, covering the well-kept green lawns with thick summer snow. I waded through it, picked it up and threw it around. Our hosts rolled their eyes. They said it gets in the drains and causes all sorts of mischief. I can smell it now too, the fragrance that filled the air, bringing me back to long afternoon shadows on those lawns, Adirondack chairs, lakes and harbours, Halifax beer and lobster. I don't remember much of anything; how do I remember that?

Why is Azalea a black cottonwood? Black cottonwood trees are rare here. It used to be said that people became trees that suited the area where they dug in, but that theory is largely discredited. Did Azalea ever visit Nova Scotia? When did I? Or have I imagined it? Invented it?

Did we ever spend a summer in Nova Scotia? I write to Caelyn.

Not that I remember.

Where are you?

Osaka.

I scroll through my old photos. There it is, a few years ago, a field of cottonwood fluff, Caelyn smiling in front of a lobster and an Adirondack chair looking out at the sea. Smiles, happiness, sunshine. It all comes back. Caelyn had presented at a conference in Halifax, back in the early days of her career when that was exciting. We were happy and content. She'd found her path, but no-one knew who she was. There were no expectations or obligations. Travel was a thing we did because we could, not because we had to. When she published the book, everything changed. She was in demand. Her career and her life became thrilling and full of promise, but out of control. It was like we were skiing on a run that was too steep for us. Or maybe just for me. I close the laptop. Looking at old photos is too close. It brings fidelity to moments that have long drifted away. Good memories are always painful, always simmering with what has since been lost. Better to let them go.

I think about her dark red hair. I twist it around my fingers, kiss her skull, wrap my arms around her. 'And it's gone,' I say to no-one, 'and it's gone.'

Late at night.
I'm tired, Bren.
So come home.
There's no home left.
I know.

We need a scissor lift to access the top branches of a struggling acacia, but we can't get one because several operators in the city have become trees. The remaining companies are struggling to keep up with the demand. Instead, George climbs to the top with a harness and spurs, apologising to the tree – Clarissa – every time he shoves his spurs into her bark.

Over a video call, I show Caelyn the trunk of the red gum. It's taken root easily enough out here in the hills, not far from the city. It was once a sixty-year-old woman whose Aboriginal ancestry tied her to this place but who grew up separated from it.

She says, 'She's progressed into full arborescence. Healthy enough. Might just be a weird-looking tree.'

'Really?' I say, pointing the camera to a section of the trunk that looks like the face of a screaming woman. 'She looks in pain.'

'Bren, you know that's not her face,' she says. 'She's doing fine.'

'How do you know?'

'I don't. But lots of trunks have naturally occurring patterns that look vaguely human-like.'

I show her again. It's uncanny, and remarkably like the face of the woman in the photo her sister gave me. 'Really?'

'Really.'

—

'We're actually counsellors, not arborists,' George says.

'I dunno,' I say. 'I think we're more like funeral directors. We make sure the bodies clean up alright. We're there for the living more than the, um, inanimate.'

He nods. 'As I said when you started, this isn't death,' he says. 'But I take your point.'

Travis says, 'Mum, you can't go.'

She doesn't respond.

We are sitting beside her in the backyard, drinking coffee. She has been standing there for days.

'She's given up,' Travis says.

'That's not what this is,' I say.

Travis looks at me with his eyes full of tears and says, 'So what the fuck is it? What the fuck is it, Bren?'

She's soaked, her hair is matted, her skin is red, her eyes are closed and her arms are by her side. From her bare feet, small roots reach into the ground, anchoring her. If we tried to pick her up now, we'd need a saw. It would hurt. It might kill her. And it wouldn't stop anything for long. Most people who have been removed from the kinetic phase and survive find another opportunity eventually.

'All I know is that she's been content for a while,' I say. 'She hasn't given up. She believes in something.'

'Like what?'

I think for a moment. This has been happening to her for years. It's been happening to us for years. There's only so much energy to go around. We're in a room with no exits and limited oxygen. It was always going to happen, this correction. I'm surprised at how gentle it is. It's a calm but unsettling rebalancing. It hurts, it takes, and those of us who remain are left with enormous grief. But it's not death. It's not a sudden, great, cataclysmic end. If it eventually comes for us all, if the entire planet becomes covered with our wooden bones and new shoots, if the world goes back to green and sky, would it be so bad? Or if it eventually stops, and whoever is left has to relearn how to live, would that be so bad? It's all seemed so sad to me until now. It had felt like extinction. But maybe it's not. Maybe it's the best possible outcome. Maybe Caelyn's been right all along.

'I reckon she believes in the future,' I say.

He looks at me with his big sad eyes and says, 'But what about now? What about us?'

I put my arms around him and he releases all the air in his lungs.

—

I see what you and George and others like you are doing and I feel hopeful, Caelyn writes.

We mostly just talk to trees, you know.

She sends a laughing/crying face. A few minutes later, she writes, *Even so. Thank you.*

—

The reporter observes that Caelyn has recently stopped advocating for a non-interventionist approach to arborescence. 'You've even been supporting research into cures, despite saying previously that this was not a condition that needed a cure.'

'Yes,' she says slowly. 'I wouldn't say I've changed my mind completely. But a friend got through to me. After many attempts.' She smiles. 'Knowing him, he's oblivious to it. And I still think what is happening is part of a correction that is overdue. But . . . maybe we're worth saving.' She raises her eyebrows and looks pointedly at the camera. 'Some of us.'

They both laugh.

—

Early in his career, Irving Shrike described Voidstar as an exploration of imagination. He was surprised by the interest in it. People tried to apply meanings to its plotless storylines; he rejected them. 'It is like life,' he said, 'there is no meaning. Despite what we like to think; despite the false shapes we give to it.' He quoted Camus a lot. In his last interview, Shrike was asked why he thought Voidstar was meaningless. He gave a response that confused many, including me.

'I was young,' he said. 'I didn't know what I was talking about. I thought back then that the truth of an indifferent universe was hopeful. Better than these organised religions, spitting out their mythologies and ideologies, killing each other over what some ghost said to another ghost. But I'm older. Less arrogant, maybe. I understand religion is simply people trying to find their answer. And it's hard, in this life. We're so curious, so insistent that there must be a reason, a purpose. There must be an answer, right? Now, I believe that life is the answer to its own question. That's what I was writing about. That's what *Voidstar* is. Life answering itself.'

—

George walks around Mum and says, 'Yes, she's doing fine.' He peers at a leaf that's sprung from a new shoot on her cheek. 'Another jacaranda,' he says. 'Been a lot of those lately.'

—

It's hard to know whether the sounds that come from her are creaks of branches and boughs or groans of pain as air is exhaled over twisting, unnaturally extended vocal cords.

—

Travis makes three gin and tonics. He sets one down next to her. The roots have formed properly now and her body is slowly being swallowed by bark and branches. The blood has drained from her face. Travis picks up her glass and is about to pour it over her roots, but I grab his hand.

'Trav, no – the alcohol.'

He stops and considers the glass. 'Ah, fuck this,' he says, hurling the glass at the fence.

Henry, who's been standing vigil next to Mum whenever it's not raining, darts back inside.

'She never even drank any of my wine,' he says.

I remind him that he made her buy it, and he shakes his head and leaves.

ARBORESCENCE

Two hours later he returns. He says he needs a moment, so I give him one. After some time he comes back inside and says, 'I'm done with it. She's done. Let me know when she's . . . you know . . . and we can have a fucking wake or whatever.'

'She's not dying, Trav,' I say.

'Fine, we'll have a slumber party or a bloody spring flower festival – just let me know.'

'She's still here.'

His face contorts in anger. 'She's not fucking here,' he says. 'Whatever that is, it's not her. It's a fucking nightmare and I don't want any part of it. Couldn't even say goodbye to us, couldn't even give us a reason. Couldn't even be arsed letting us know why.'

'She said she believed in the future,' I say.

'That doesn't make any sense,' he says, and storms out.

—

One night the groans stop, but I can hear the crackling of wood and growth, bursting, thickening, reaching. For much of the night, it feels like a gentle earthquake is shaking the house, as her roots take hold, dig deep.

—

I put my hand on a thick tree trunk with at least seventy years' growth. It reaches nearly fifteen metres into the sky, towering over the little houses in the suburb, even the two-storey ones. It's a grand old tree, a spectacular jacaranda. Mum can no longer be seen. Henry lies in the sun at her feet and occasionally rubs his back against her bark.

'Looks like you're done,' I say. 'Alright, Mum. Alright.'

—

On windy days I will hear the creak of her branches. I will see the delicate yellow-green buds in spring, the resplendent purple flowers in summer, sprinkling their colour everywhere.

—

I go through her study, Travis' old bedroom, filled with paintings by Turner and Monet. Mum loved the way they represented light. She said she found it comforting, or spiritual, or something. I find a quote she's written down on a notepad next to a list of her favourite songs.

It's terrible how the light runs out, taking colour with it.

I remember back to those evenings, sunset-washed, gin-hazed, when we would sit and watch as the day faded. She would say, 'The light always runs out,' as if I knew what she meant. Next to the notepad, a few pamphlets from an organisation promoting arborescence as a way of combatting climate guilt. There, too, folders with brochures of European travel, trips she could never afford to take. Trips I never offered to take her on, even when I could afford to, while I was flitting about the world, sending her photos from Rome, from France, from everywhere she dreamed of going, as if to say, *See? Look at what you'll never do.*

ARBORESCENCE

'FUCK!' I scream, dropping to my knees, then punching the carpet and hurting my hand. I punch it again anyway. Why didn't I why didn't I why didn't I fuck fuck fuck fuck fuck.

—

Henry hasn't moved from the base of the tree for days. There's no evidence that cats can become trees, but I'm pretty sure he's trying. Eventually he comes inside to eat, and sits on my lap as I watch an old episode of *Lawn Kings of Boca Raton*.

'You're still here, buddy,' I say.

He stares through the window at the tree.

'Yeah, I know. But we're what's left now.'

He closes his eyes and we settle in for the evening.

—

'It's still grief,' George says. 'The trees don't care, not in the way they would have when they were human, but we do, you know? Take a few weeks off. I'll be fine.'

—

We hold a ceremony in the backyard. Her friends come from all over the state to sit beneath her boughs. Her purple flowers blossom a few days before, almost as if she'd planned it. We laugh and play her favourite music and drink her favourite gin. It's early December and the sun is warm and she filters it softly, protecting her people, her flock. Travis and I sing along to 'Hey Jude' a few times. Her friends hug us, not sure whether to offer condolences or congratulations. They pat her bark. Some of them cry next to her. The day sparkles.

In the late afternoon, I hear a familiar but distant voice.

'Bren,' Ray says. 'I'd really like to speak to you.'

My heart sinking, I turn to face Miles's father.

'Okay,' I say. 'Okay.'

'Your mother is a wonderful woman,' he says. 'Take My Breath Away' by Berlin plays in the background, and Travis sings it at Shakti, who is talking to one of mum's friends and waves him away.

'Thanks, Ray,' I say.

'She never forgot about us,' he says. 'Everyone else did, after those first six months. But she never left us. Always called by to check in.'

'Ray,' I say, 'I never forgot about Miles.'

He shakes his head. 'Not what I'm saying, mate. You were a kid. You grew apart. Not up to you. I just want you to know how much she did for us.'

'I just don't think he needed me around.'

He nods sadly and looks up at the sky. 'A few of us felt that way. His journal. You left it for us, I think,' he says. 'It helped me come to terms. I reckon there's a few pages you should read. Won't give you any answers, but it might help.' He reaches into his pocket and pulls out a few folded pieces of paper, handing them to me. 'My boy was ahead of his time.' He smiles, squeezes my shoulder and moves away.

The world keeps slowing down. Glorious shafts of light filter through bright leaves and branches; the air, clean and pure; the light, always the light, as if I've never seen it before. The colour always runs out, Mum said, and yet, here it is, at all times of the day, so much colour everywhere.

—

I drop by Neko's to say hello. He says his mother died. I say I'm sorry.

'She shouldn't have died,' he says. 'It's all these, all this.' He waves at the sky. 'Weren't any bloody ambulances. Couldn't even get a cab or a driver to her. I'm standing there behind that fucking espresso machine and my mother is dying and I can't do a fucking thing about it.'

'Shit, Neko,' I say, 'that's horrible.'

'Yeah,' he says. 'All due respect, but words don't do much.'

I nod and look at the ground.

'Look at this place,' he says.

I follow his gaze to the street. Trees are everywhere: on the top of buildings, growing out of windows, in the middle of the road.

'It doesn't work,' he says. 'None of this works. What a shitshow. Look at this idiot, trying to drive through it.'

We watch a man in an orange car weave slowly between the trees and root-lifted asphalt.

'No point, man!' Neko shouts. 'No point! Just get out and walk!'

The man in the car gives him the finger and carries on driving slowly over kerbs and roots and median strips.

'He should just walk,' I say.

'Selfish cunts everywhere,' Neko says.

'I'm sorry about your mum,' I say.

He looks back at me with sudden recognition. 'Yeah,' he says, 'yeah. Sorry about yours too.'

'Reckon it's different,' I say.

'Maybe,' he says, 'but not to you.'

The cafe is closed for good three days later.

—

Driverless cars going in circles around roundabouts, or driving on highways outside of the city, going as far as they can before running out of petrol. Queues of them outside charging stations, waiting for a friendly human to plug them in. Drones dropping from the sky, sputtering in fields, in parks, on rooftops or stuck in trees.

ARBORESCENCE

—

After meeting with a family who is disappointed their father has become a melaleuca rather than something more significant, like a mountain ash or an oak, I go to a pub to meet Travis. While I'm waiting, I rifle through my backpack for something to doodle on. I find the pages that Ray gave me. I must have put them in there at Mum's ceremony without thinking. I'd forgotten about them. I try not to think about what that says about me, and inspect the pages. There are three of them, all photocopied from different parts of Miles's journal.

I've never been in control. Mum and Dad have always done their best, but it's never been enough. It doesn't feel like anything good is coming. The world is dying. We can't stop it. All we do is talk. We're fucking useless. How good would it be if we could just stop everything. Just stop. Stay still for a while. Give the planet a chance to catch up. It's crazy, what these people are saying up here. Turn into a tree, give life back to the burning world. It's not real. It can't be real. Right? But even if it isn't, I'd like to just stand still for a while. To take control by losing control. To make a fucking difference.

Fuck I was an arsehole. I loved so many people who I treated like shit. Mum, Dad, Pat, Quinn, Bren, my teachers. I'm sorry. I don't know what happened. Something switched off in me. I don't know what it was, but it was there one day and gone the next. There are people here who have become trees. For real. I can't explain it.

It's fucking crazy. I'm going to give it a go soon. If any of you ever see this, if it works, I want you to know: it's because I love you.

The last page is a drawing of a redwood forest with a single caption: *Voidstar #273*. I don't remember the issue.

Travis messages to say Cal is sick so he can't come to the pub. His three kids have sickness on a rotating schedule.

I finish my beer and head back home, where I find my old box of *Voidstar* comics. After a bit of searching, I find number 273, a little tattered. On the cover, the crowns of a redwood forest. It's titled *Into the Arboretum*. As I flick through the comic, my heart beats quickly.

Voidstar, in the form of an ordinary human, decides in the first few pages to become a seedling in a sleek, futuristic city. The entire comic is then devoted to an exploration of tree-time, in which bizarre big-eyed animals pass by, in which seasons become moments, in which music flies on the air, in which spores and gases and electricity swirl and, slowly, slowly, the reaching down, the reaching up, the reaching out to siblings, the growing, the calling. A road cuts through, a road breaks apart. A fire erupts, a fire goes out. In tree-time, Voidstar stays for centuries.

I remember being disappointed with this one, so I gave it to Miles. I got it back when his parents gave me his collection.

After Voidstar changes to a tree, the panels become black and empty, populated only with captions. We never know exactly what's happening, we only get a sense of vibrations, of strange, uncanny sensations. In the last panel, however, we pan out to see an enormous tree at the centre of a forest that has taken over a ruined city. If you look close enough you can see a few warm lights from a few small villages scattered through the forest. It's an extraordinary image, filled with colour and detail: flocks of birds, approaching rain, and many types of trees growing in incongruous places, from balconies, from the roofs of cars.

I stare at it for a long, long time.

—

In that final interview, Irving Shrike also said he was aware of the prescience of some of his comics, but that when you make thousands of predictions of the future, you're bound to get a couple right. *The Simpsons* has a better strike rate, he said, laughing.

The media tells us that the GDP is collapsing at a rate never seen before.

Caelyn tells an economist that we need different measures. 'Growth,' she says, 'is irrelevant in a human system that is no longer growing. Never mind the robots.' I catch a half-smile flitting across her face.

The interviewer is thrown but follows up with another question. 'What measures do you suggest?'

But she's lost in thought. She looks bored again. She's not changing anything. She's been doing this for years now, explaining what she can, placating, arguing. Appearing on podcasts or news channels, delivering lectures, always moving, never stopping. She lives in New York but tells me she's rarely there.

The interviewer repeats her name.

'Sorry,' she says. 'I'm no economist.'

The economist on the panel says, 'Exactly.'

Caelyn's expression hardens and she snaps back to life. 'But I'd suggest my friend here study degrowth economic principles. Like most of her colleagues have been doing for some time.'

The economist actually says, 'Bah.'

Caelyn continues, 'I would start, for example, with Professor Dominique Maille, whose book . . .'

Someone says hello in the real world. I stop the video and put my phone down.

'Hello,' I say, looking up to see a woman, mid-forties, with short brown hair and glasses.

'Bren?' she says, and I say, 'Yes. Amelia?'

She says yes and sits down at the table in the cafe. We talk and it's not awful, and we eat and it's fairly decent, and by the end we're still talking, so we go to a bar, and after a few drinks we're still talking, and she says that I'm not terrible to look at, and I say she's surprisingly attractive, considering, and we laugh and she invites me back to her place.

She says, as we're rolling around, 'It's nice, this easy kind of thing, isn't it?'

I say, 'Yes, it's nice.'

'I'm so sick of drama,' she says.

'Who needs drama?' I say. 'It's so much nicer this way. And easier.'

I don't stay. I walk home, my entire body aching.

At home I stand in the shower for far too long, drinking the hot water. I don't think you're supposed to do that, but the alcohol and the sex has made me thirsty.

—

I know what this means.

I want to rest on rich, sunlit soil.

Yes, I know what this means.

—

I've been thinking about it all wrong. We're not losing anything. The world is flowering. The air is full of perfume. All these connections that appear and disappear, all this pace, all this movement. We don't need any of it. Just the wind to take our sighs and signals where it will. There's a fabric, a weave, a network, a something more, a something we were always part of. There is no difference between animals and plants, we're in it together, they are helping us, we are helping them, pushing back the void, pushing back the cold, pushing back the desolate, together in life, together in death, growing, reaching out, reaching up, reaching down, together.

—

I go back to work. I read a poem to Eileen, a Japanese maple. She was once a yoga instructor and wellness coach who sold arboreal alliance kits. She promised her clients the product would help them feel more connected to those they'd lost to arborescence but would also prevent it from occurring to them.

After I finish, I sit on a bench and watch hundreds of monarch butterflies flutter across the park. I can hear them if I listen hard enough.

A few hours later I wake up to a message from George.

How you going out there? Haven't heard from you.

Sorry, I write back, *this place is beautiful. Butterflies and sunshine everywhere. Job's done, accidentally fell asleep. Will make up some time tomorrow.*

Nah, he messages, *as long as you're alright.*

—

Henry stretches his weary old bones in front of me. He makes his way slowly onto the couch, headbutts me a few times, then, after thoroughly testing the cushions, curls up beside me. His spine rests against my leg and I scratch his ribs gently. We stay like that as it gets darker and the lights go on in the street: silent, still, keeping each other warm as the night gets colder.

When I wake sometime early in the morning, he doesn't. He stays frozen, curled up against my leg.

I pick him up, hold him, and weep for him, for my mother, for my father, for Travis and Caelyn and Miles and Shakti, I weep like I should weep every fucking day, hard and shuddering and emptying; I weep the way we should all be weeping, for the loss of everything and everyone, for the void and the warmth and the alone, for the collapse and bombs and little animals scurrying, hiding, pretending, trying to communicate, trying to say no, no thanks, I don't want that, I want to live, I want to stay, and their little spines and little paws, and all of it gone, all of it going, and I cannot stop any of it, and I am so goddamn sick I am so sick of it let it be done then let it be over let our legacy hang in the air like a great stinking cloud of sulphur and ash, let us sink and be done.

He was old, I tell myself. He was tired. His legs were always sore, even if he wouldn't admit it. He was black and white and had golden eyes that shone bright in the sunlight he craved.

I am so sorry, my beautiful little boy.

I dig a hole in the earth next to Mum, among the roots she has formed. The earth, the air, the sky. In the dawn light, I lay Henry down, I give him back, and the sun rises as if fully aware of how it should be worshipped, streaking through clouds, shimmering the spires, shedding itself, burning itself brilliant.

———

Caelyn closes her social media accounts overnight. She stops doing interviews. I message her a few times but she doesn't answer. I stop trying. She doesn't have to explain herself.

———

I spend an afternoon reading messages and playing songs to a family of poplars in wine country, not far from Travis's place, and head home a little drunk and weary. I crawl into bed at 6 pm with a litre of water. I put *Brick Barons of Lantz* on to try to stay awake, but it doesn't help, and I sleep until the 11 pm news bulletin blares across the screen, screaming about fires and a UN conference on arborescence in Cairo.

I go out onto the deck and look up at Mum reaching for the stars. Even the great milky firmament seems tiny against the ocean of dark, of cold, of void. We are barely here, an unlikely anomaly, a strange planet full of life only just holding on. It's so tenuous. It's so implausible. I stay outside until the sun comes up. In the dawn I watch the flowers bloom all over the city.

ARBORESCENCE

I fall dreamlessly asleep to the sound of the wind and the scent of a thousand different perfumes.

―

All is not lost, it says.

―

I wake on a hill overlooking the city. We used to come here for the view, hardly a blink ago. We would eat and drink with friends I've long since lost touch with and watch the city lights, next to the Norfolk pines standing heavy and tall against the fierce southern winds, and I'm here, next to them, and I'm not sure if they want me here, but I'm here, in the soil, in the air. I attempt to make a wry observation, but I'm not sure if I make a sound.

―

I want to stay here. I want to know this place as it passes through years of sunlight and moonlight, through winters and long summers. Here, I'll stand guard over the city that made me. I will hold tight to the earth, and I will stretch toward the sun, and I will let the wind shake my limbs and take me where it will.

This is where it will be.

―

All is not lost, it says.

Air and wind. Sun and stars. Crackling of earth and root. Here we go. Here we stay. Continuing. Becoming. Returning. Stilling. This was the place. A place. Not *the* place. Just the place I happened to land. A hard place, a cold place. With skin and bark and fingers and limbs. A face, I remember a face, a sight, an understanding of where they were, where I was, and how we would move together, how we would move, but not now.

—

Pain, muscles tearing, hardening, thickening, pain, sounds scarcely heard.

—

We will flow like sparks across currents of air, of water, of stellar light. We will start, somewhere. We will grow, somehow. We will move, in our way, together. Through soundwaves, through flowers and roots and feather and skin and scales and bone, through earth and atmosphere, we will move, we will cast ourselves to the roaring winds, to time. Some will buzz, some will crawl, some dig, some sway. Together we will be more than we are. Life, bursting, digging, holding fast. We will resist entropy, we will persist. All is not lost, we will say, when all seems lost.

—

Some sounds, still. Some light, still. But different. Not better, not worse.

Beasts arrive and circle.
Looks late kinetic, early dormant-transitory, the vibration says.
He's too far gone, says another.
No.

In the end, they thought it was better not to announce it.
Why not?
We might not be able to make enough.
Do you think this is what he wants?
Probably not. But I can't . . . he can't.

Vibrations murmuring. The crackling of a fire. Influx of chemicals. Fear, of a kind. I send out a warning to those around me. They send it further. Warnings through the earth, through the atmosphere.

Not you, the vibration says. *Not you.*

A beast at my feet, curled up, dormant. Sleep, beast. You are tired. Sleep. Perhaps to expire there and nourish the earth.

Chemicals. Warning. Changing, not changing. Reversing, reducing. Softening. I can feel the air on my bones. Something's wrong. This is not the way there.

The sound of her voice, singing. I can't remember the song, but I remember that I should.

An orange light growing brighter. My eyelids feel like they're glued shut. I open them with effort. A campfire, a sunset, a blinking city, a tent, a red-grey-haired woman turning, a look, a gasp, her arms, her hair, we are moving, we are moving again.

It's a week before I can move. Caelyn says she doesn't want to risk any more shock. She helps me shuffle to a large tent with a skylight. I lie there and watch the stars swing by. My bones creak, my muscles ache, my skin screams. She makes me eat, applies ointments, gives me painkillers and concoctions full of nutrients she says my animal body has been missing. She writes notes and performs rudimentary tests. She says this is new, and that she's sorry it hurts. I can tell she wants to know all about it, but I'm not sure I want to tell her.

It's as if my body is shedding a skin, an idea, a way of being. It hurts, until it hurts less, and I can sit up, and I can control my vocal cords, and I can stand, and I can, slowly, walk. But I was so close.

—

With difficulty, I say, 'I was so close.'

She hands me a cup of tea and shakes her head. 'I know,' she says. 'I didn't . . . I couldn't.'

'You didn't. You couldn't.'

'Yes. I'm sorry.'

'Not an explanation.'

'I couldn't. Not you. And yes, I'm aware I'm a hypocrite. I know. I'm sorry. But not you, Bren. I would have . . . lost hope.'

'Haven't been together for years.'

'Still,' she says.

—

She moves the same way. The smell of her skin, when she comes close enough, is the same as it was. Her smile is sadder, perhaps, but it's the same smile.

—

Sometimes I catch something on the air I don't recognise. Something new, or new to me, or new to this version of me. Has my memory been altered, or are these new things I can detect?

—

'How did you do this? How is this even possible?'

'One of the labs has released some prototypes. I was helping with the effort. Tracking recovery, conducting interviews to make sure it was safe, that sort of thing. Travis got in touch, said they found you digging in here. He was desperate, Bren. I didn't hesitate.'

'Does he know? That I'm still here?'

'He knows. Probably isn't going to talk to you for a while.'

'I guess I wasn't thinking about . . . other people.' I scratch my forearm. The skin remains rough. 'I'm not the first to have it reversed?'

'No. There've been a few. It's being kept very quiet for now.'

She inspects my arm and runs her hand along the remaining bark-like sections. 'Some of this might not heal. But most of it should. They think it's linked to an ancient genetic code. There may be a link to a common ancestor. Perhaps not far from the beginning of life itself.'

'I said that years ago,' I say. 'When we found Miles. You told me that's not how it works.'

She looks at me sceptically. 'Well, there've been a lot of theories. We have some proof now though. We don't know what triggers it, but we've worked out how to tell it to back off. Just a matter of whether we want to, and whether we can make enough.'

'Should we?'

'Yes,' she says, 'I think we should.'

'You've changed your tune,' I say.

'Maybe,' she says, marking something down in her notebook.

'I assume you're writing that I told you the answer years ago and you arrogantly overlooked my insight.'

'I've been known to overlook things,' she says, and gently turns my forearm to inspect the other side.

—

She continues taking notes and running tests.

I don't tell her everything. I don't tell her about the whispers, not in any language that I know, that are still buzzing through my blood. But I don't think she's telling me everything either.

———

George visits and says he wasn't going to stop her. I say he couldn't if he tried. He says it's nice to have me back.

———

Travis sends me an angry text, and I say I'm sorry, and he doesn't respond until the next day, when he says Violet, his eldest, is probably going to become a star basketball player. I say that's wonderful and that I'm sorry, and he doesn't respond until the next day, when he sends through a video of a talking goat. It goes on like this for a while.

———

One afternoon, as the sun sets, she climbs into my sleeping bag. She looks at me with those dark blue eyes. She asks me why I chose this place, this hill that we used to visit. I say that I don't know, but chances are it might be my favourite place. She smiles and says, 'Might be.'

'Might be,' I say. 'Can't say for sure.' She puts her hand on my cheek. She kisses my lips and lingers there for a while. She breathes and I breathe and we move together.

Afterward I say, 'Mum said our relationship was unhealthy.'

'I don't think anything's as unhealthy as fucking someone who was nearly a tree. We should leave soon. Take you home.'

'Okay,' I say.

'Okay,' she says.

I decide to say what I mean. 'Once we pack up, I'd like it if you stayed for a while,' I say.

'Well,' she says, 'Maybe I could. Just for a while.'

'Just for a while,' I say.

'Just for a while,' she says.

—

We pack up. My body still hurts. It may hurt for a long time. We don't know.

'You used to be able to hear the hum of traffic from here,' she says.

'We're losing the war,' I say.

Before us, the sun slips down over verdant city streets. A world of green and orange and yellow, of eucalypt, myrtle, oak, cedar, cypress, plane, willow, dogwood, frangipani, maple, acacia, palm, pine, elm, apple, boab, mahogany, jacaranda, cottonwood, sycamore, alder, ash, grevillea, chestnut, poplar, birch, on streets, on football ovals, growing from abandoned cars and front yards and cafes and train stations.

'I don't think it's a fight,' she says.

We're talking about different wars. She's talking about a war between trees and humans. That's not what I mean. In my war, the trees are on our side. The enemy is unseen, cold, empty, infinite. It's a war against death. But this is also something I don't want to tell her yet. 'No, maybe not,' I say.

She turns to me and narrows her eyes. 'That was a test to see what side you're on. And that's exactly what one of them would say.'

I shrug.

She gasps. 'I knew it,' she says. 'You're a collaborator.' She points a finger gun at me.

I laugh and put my hands up. 'Off to the salt mines then,' I say.

I look back at the city. One day, it will again be a garden. It is as inevitable as it will be beautiful. I can see it. Once electric lights, once people, once human chaos and concrete, once earthmoving and shaking. Then still. The buildings, once full, empty. Weeds and bushes and trees will burst from rooftops, through windows. What was once a dazzling metropolis will be an arboretum, a forest of millions of trees. There will be a few pockets of warm light where small communities remain, still moving, still there, still talking, still learning. And up, and out, beyond the garden city, to the bright country, to the green-blue planet spinning in darkness. This is where we will be. We will be our own answer.

She shoots. I collapse to the ground. She whispers into my shocked, dying face, 'Collaborators are shot on sight.'

I shudder a few times, draw out my death scene, and expire. I stay dead for as long as I can. When I open my eyes, she's standing over me. 'Come on,' she says, 'I'll drive you to Travis and Shakti's.'

'Seems right,' I say. She helps me up.

We drive away in silence. Somewhere between where we started and where we're going, the road bisects a small forest of eucalypts. Their arms reach out to each other across the asphalt, swaying, creaking, conversing in the breeze. Through the canopy, colour and sound and mist rise to meet the sky. Through the canopy, the world brims with an unusual light.

ACKNOWLEDGEMENTS

This novel was largely written on the lands of the Wadawurrung and the Wurundjeri of the Kulin nation.

A few small fragments were adapted from 'Straight to You', a short story I published in *Into Your Arms: Nick Cave's Songs Reimagined*, from Fremantle Press.

Endless thanks to: Rebecca Allen, Momo Chavez, Maddie Garratt, Vanessa Radnidge and all at Hachette Australia, Josh Baird, Rob Browning, Alexandra Christie and Curtis Brown Australia, Caz Copic and Gillian Elijah at Geelong Regional Libraries, Chris Flynn, Clare Forster, Charlotte Guest, Rebecca Hamilton, Alice Hoskyns and C&W Agency, Jeremy Lachlan, Ali Lavau, Kate Mildenhall, Ben Rawlence, Mark Mupotsa-Russell, Inga Simpson, Matilda Singer and all at Fleet in the UK, Anna Tweed, and many others I've probably forgotten to mention.

Thanks also to my family: Jenny Davis (you would have liked this one), Ken Davis (not as sure but I remain hopeful), Lorraine Jennings, Ben Davis, Brooke Davis, Tara Coady, the Coady family, Barbara Headlam, and Lenny, Maple and Manu.

Lastly, thanks to those I've lost along the way.

Arborescence owes its existence to a childhood spent near the grand coastal forests of south-western Victoria, from the Ironbark Basin to the Otways. These forests were guarded for tens of thousands of years by the Wadawurrung and the Gadubanud people but are now bafflingly precarious. If we lose these forests – and those like them around the world – we lose ourselves. May they always reach for the unusual light.

Rhett Davis is from the Wadawurrung Country of Geelong and its nearby coastal towns. His debut novel, *Hovering*, won the Victorian Premier's Literary Award for an Unpublished Manuscript in 2020, and was shortlisted for the Readings Prize for New Australian Fiction and the Aurealis Award for Best Science Fiction. Rhett lives in Geelong with his partner and two talkative cats.

Find Rhett Davis on Instagram: @rhettsdavis

RAISING READERS
Books Build Bright Futures

Dear Reader,

We'd love your attention for one more page to tell you about the crisis in children's reading, and what we can all do.

Studies have shown that reading for fun is the **single biggest predictor of a child's future life chances** – more than family circumstance, parents' educational background or income. It improves academic results, mental health, wealth, communication skills, ambition and happiness.[1]

The number of children reading for fun is in rapid decline. Young people have a lot of competition for their time. In 2024, 1 in 10 children and young people in the UK aged 5 to 18 did not own a single book at home.[2]

Hachette works extensively with schools, libraries and literacy charities, but here are some ways we can all raise more readers:

- Reading to children for just 10 minutes a day makes a difference
- Don't give up if children aren't regular readers – there will be books for them!
- Visit bookshops and libraries to get recommendations
- Encourage them to listen to audiobooks
- Support school libraries
- Give books as gifts

There's a lot more information about how to encourage children to read on our website: **www.RaisingReaders.co.uk**

Thank you for reading.

[1] OECD, '21st-Century Readers: Developing Literacy Skills in a Digital World', 2021, https://www.oecd.org/en/publications/21st-century-readers_a83d84cb-en.html

[2] National Literacy Trust, 'Book Ownership in 2024', November 2024, https://literacytrust.org.uk/research-services/research-reports/book-ownership-in-2024